The Quest for Redefining Oneself

Alka Sharma

Contents

Chapter-1

Conquer your fear

It was drizzling outside. Lost in my thoughts, I was trying to lookout of the window of the airbus which was partially covered with trails of water droplets. As the plane took off, my memories unknowingly flew me back to my past, which I had left way behind.

Sixteen years back, I was wiping the window pane of my car to get rid of the fog which was repeatedly obscuring my vision. It was raining heavily. Looking at the intensity of rain, I was getting worried for my dog house as it was in need of some urgent repairs. I was not sure, whether it would stand this havoc or not.

While sitting on the back seat of our car; I wished that instead of travelling in such a bad weather, we should have stayed back at home and enjoyed a cup of hot coffee with a bowl of spicy snacks.

However, far from the comfort of home, our car was heading towards my new school "The Convent of Hills" where I was about to be enrolled for class 10th. Within a few hours, I would be another hosteller lodged with unknown people in a completely new place.

I took note of my mother's facial expressions who was sitting beside me. A tinge of happiness doused by anxiety was very much evident over her face.

It was one of the most prestigious schools and an alma mater to many successful people ranging from politicians to business tycoons. Getting admission in this school was not an easy task but adjusting to the new school's environment was much scarier thought in itself. The most daunting task was to pretend that everything is fine and there is nothing to worry about.

No matter how hard I tried to distract myself but my mother kept reminding me that I am going to enter a new school and in a new phase of life. So, she advised me to keep myself disciplined, stay away from unnecessary brawls and focus equally on studies as well as sports.

I was nodding in affirmation to her because at that point of time this was the only answer expected from me. In reality, I never excelled in sports but my dad always wanted me to play basketball for the school. I was very much confident that this dream will never see the light of reality because playing basketball was way beyond my capabilities.

Still, I never asked them to stop dreaming and be optimistic about me. At least in their imagination, they can be gratified by me.

It was not that I didn't like games or I never tried playing. But whenever I did, it was extremely difficult for me to get hold of the ball.

In one such terribly memorable inter–house basketball match in my previous school, I was able to touch the ball only twice during the entire game. Unluckily, I moved to the scoring position and finding me there, one idiot from my team hurled the ball towards me. The moment I got hold of the ball, the players of the opposite team raided me like an army platoon attacking the enemy country.

In the rest of the match, I never wished for the ball to even come closer to me. In-fact, I tried my best to stay as far as possible from the ball and scoring positions.

Quite understandably, the coach decided to drop me from the team and never reconsidered me. I never felt bad for this, but my dad did. Well, what could have been done? Practically it wasn't possible for me to repeatedly face the fear of ball followed by bullying.

However, today the matter was altogether different. I was about to meet the next most feared thing of my life - a new Headmaster. I was praying and wishing for some miracle to save me from the unpleasant.

With sudden deluge of rain, it was becoming impossible for the driver to manoeuver the car any further. Therefore, we decided to halt for a while and wait for the weather to clear up before moving any further. We were lucky enough to spot a restaurant nearby. Although it was not a fancy one but considering the weather condition we decided to stop there for a coffee.

The restaurant was very shoddy in appearance. The manager was sitting on a creaky chair with a very mundane expression as if he has nothing to do with this business. We were greeted by his old waiter with a big toothless smile. The duo appeared to have been handpicked for the job.

Once the rain transformed to drizzle, we continued with our journey. On our way to the school, we came across a narrow gauge railway track which was running parallel to the road and the view was spectacular. To me it appeared as if the railway line and the road were racing against each other. I enjoyed this view for a few kilometers but my state of exhilaration dampened a little when the railway tracks entered into a tunnel only not to reappear again to my view and left the road all alone by itself.

Although we were on the right track, my father still preferred enquiring about the directions to the school from a group of people standing at the crossroads.

As we advanced further, he said while describing the school to us, "This is a reputed school with strict educational norms. It has a well-experienced faculty and a vast campus."

He continued with a spontaneous smile, "They also have a recognized sports team. This is exactly the kind of school we were looking for our son. Isn't it ... Sunaina?"

My mother nodded in affirmation and replied "Yes, indeed Ravi" while she gently caressed my hairs out of affection (although I had to re-comb them afterwards). "One day our son would be a star sportsman" she added. Her statement amused me; therefore I tried to shift their focus on to the rain that was not showing any sign of weaning. The school was situated at the hilltop; therefore, as we moved further the rain transformed into a heavy downpour. No matter how hard it rained, we made it to the school.

The school had tall gates and there was a security post at the gate. Probably, due to heavy rains no one was standing outside the post. Therefore, our driver had to blow horn to seek attention of the security guards. Sighting our car, a guard came out of his cabin, holding an umbrella in his hand and asked my father, "Sir, what brings you here? May I see your identity proof"?

My father replied while showing him his visiting card, "We are here for the admission of our son. We are having an appointment with your Headmaster at 2.00 pm".

The guard went inside, quickly checked his register and said after returning to us, "Sure sir, you do have an appointment with the Headmaster. You can proceed". (He opened the main gate for us and let our vehicle pass through. Our driver stopped the car at the porch. Finally, we stepped out of the car and walked towards my new school.)

The first thing to catch attention was a magnificent reception hall at the school entrance. The hall was connected to the rest of school buildings by two identical corridors, placed at right angles to each other. The corridors were quite broad and built aesthetically with brick red walls and brownish floor tiles. To me, they looked more like an open verandah rather than closed and suffocating corridors.

My father enquired about the Headmaster from the receptionist. She gave us the directions towards his room and also wished me good luck.

As we walked through the corridors towards his office, I noticed several beautiful paintings placed at uniform intervals and at an identical height on the left wall of the corridor. From a distance, the paintings would appear like a group of students standing in a straight line. What a discipline! Amazingly, all of the paintings were made by the students themselves. After travelling through few intersecting corridors, we reached the Headmaster's office.

The peon informed us that the Headmaster prefers to meet the parents and the children separately before giving his consent for admission. The peon gave me directions to the visitor's canteen, whereas my parents went inside the office to meet the Headmaster.

I wasn't a very brilliant student, so I was petrified of being scolded for my average performance in academics. As a result, my imagination hibernated and suddenly the surroundings started to appear displeasing and noisy. I had ordered a burger but was finding it very unpalatable and hard to swallow. All of my hunger perished in front of the fear of facing the Headmaster all alone.

That day I realized that fear does not die with age if you keep on remaining ignorant about its cause. No matter how old you become, it keeps on growing with you unless and until you find a way to counter it. So, I was praying to God and trying my level best to manage my fear and anxiety.

After completing their important discussion with the Headmaster which lasted for half an hour, my parents joined me in the canteen and I was relieved to find that they were looking happy and content. My mother said, "Your Headmaster is quite a gentleman and he treats people with politeness and respect". I thought to myself that who would not treat a rich man like my father with respect and politeness.

She added further, "The Headmaster has made it clear to me that the school does not believe in any form of corporal punishment as it hampers the mental growth of children and also induces fear as well as violence in their minds."

It came to my mind that every Headmaster paints a rosy picture of his school in front of the parents and it is the child who receives thrashing for his or her poor performance in academics afterwards. I wondered whether what could be his method of punishment if he does not use a stick.

Dad said while placing his hand on my shoulder, "Satyam, the school would now conduct an oral and a written test before accepting you as a student of this school. Thereafter, you have a meeting with the Headmaster in his room at 4 pm. So don't be late."

I walked them up to the parking where the driver was waiting in the car. Reaching the parking lot, mother hugged me tightly while tears flowed from her eyes. Mustering courage and trying to keep all of my anxiety aside, I said assuring her, "Don't worry Mom, I'll do my best. Wish me luck."

She replied while wiping her tears, "God bless you." She held my face in her hands and kissed my forehead.

"Grades are not the only criteria to judge talent and capability. Be

confident while replying to his questions" Dad said as he placed his arm around my shoulder.

"Yes Dad", I replied as he embraced me.

Placing his hand on Mom's shoulder, he continued, "Your mother has become quite emotional. So instead of waiting in the reception area, we will wait here."

Noticing that she was trying her best to stop the tears flowing from her eyes, I hugged her again.

Mom and Dad seated themselves inside the car. I stepped aside and after waving an initial goodbye to my parents, I shifted my focus towards the new phase of my life. I was much happy to know that my parents are more concerned about me rather than my grades. Sometimes, I don't completely understand my father but he knows my mindset well.

I walked back from the parking lot towards the reception where the receptionist informed me while pointing towards a room across the reception that the examination will be conducted in room no. 32 after five minutes. I was eager as well as anxious to appear in my first ever examination in the new school.

I managed to answer nineteen out of twenty-five questions. The written test was followed by an oral test in which I fumbled ini-

tially but gradually, I gained in confidence and managed to answer almost all of the questions except for two of them. After the examination was over, the teacher appreciated me for my performance and told me to be prepared for my final interaction with the Headmaster at 4 p.m.

As I walked out of the room, I glanced at the big wall clock placed on the wall behind the reception desk. The time was quarter to four; so, I decided to walk towards the Headmaster's room which was located at the extreme corner of the left wing on the first floor. It took me almost five minutes to get there.

On reaching, I noticed a board nailed at the outer wall besides his room. Although the written text was not clearly visible from the distance I stood but as I moved closer, I could get it clearly. It read: "Questions may not be but their answers are always simple."

Meanwhile, after a brief drizzling for few hours, the rain had re-transformed into a heavy downpour. The sound of rain water bashing over the tin roof of the school building coupled with strong winds and occasional lightening were testing my already suppressed nervous state of mind.

But that day, I finally decided to overcome my fears for once and for all and give a new head start to my life.

I glanced at my watch; I was still having 10 minutes with me. Instead of pacing restlessly outside the Headmaster's room as I would have done out of anxiety, I walked calmly towards the balcony pillar. I stood there to look at the picturesque view of the landscape to de- stress my-self.

That day, I also realized that you do become what you think about yourself. Minutes ago, I was afraid of looking at the clock but now I was waiting for it to strike four.

Engrossed in my thoughts, I heard someone walking on the staircase and coming towards me. I turned around but no one was there. It was surprising because I had clearly heard the footsteps. While I was busy trying to figure out what was happening around me; suddenly, I felt something nudging against my arm.

This woke me up from the deep slumber I had gone into while looking through the window of the airbus.

It was Shreya, my wife sitting next to me. She was smiling at me.

"What?" I asked while removing my spectacles and sat upright to wipe my eyes with a handkerchief.

She said, "You dozed off while sitting. So I pulled up a blanket for you. Are you feeling fresh now?"

"Oh, yes dear", I replied as I smiled back.

"Then let's have some refreshments the air hostess had offered few minutes ago" she said.

After having some light snacks, I asked while searching for a magazine in the seat pocket, "Have you checked your hospital schedule for tomorrow?"

She replied, "Not yet. I'll contact my colleague after we reach home".

"Must be hectic, like it is always" I said.

"But I find your work taxing too. It's not an easy task to manage one's employees and keep up the reputation of the company" Shreya replied.

I said while switching on the reading light and reclining my seat, "I'll have a look at this journal meanwhile".

Shreya had accompanied me to an investor's meet in Mumbai and we were returning to our destination- New Delhi. While glancing through the journal, I spotted a weekly quiz.

The questions in the quiz drove me back to the corridor in front of the Headmaster's room where I was supposed to meet him for the first time in few minutes. While I was busy preparing myself for the upcoming interaction, I could see a boy of my age, wearing school uniform, walking towards me. He was looking quite confident. I decided to ignore him but he walked directly towards me. He greeted me with a big smile and said while stretching his hand towards me, "Hi, my name is Kartik. You must be Satyam, the new admission."

I held his hand clumsily and greeted him with a suspicious smile. "Must be the head boy or prefect of the school" I thought to myself.

"How do you know my name?" I asked surprisingly.

He replied, "The receptionist had told me that a new student is here to join our class. So I came here to greet you."

I said while looking at my watch, "It is already 4 and I am supposed to meet the Headmaster. I think I should move now."

I hurriedly turned to walk towards the Headmaster's room but in haste, failed to notice a broken tile that was lying near the pillar on the floor and tumbled upon it. I stood up as quickly as I could.

"Are you alright?" asked Kartik.

Luckily, I escaped with slight bruises on my left hand.

"I am fine. Thanks for asking" I replied while rubbing off my soiled

hand and my pants over the knees.

Kartik wished me good luck and left.

I knocked at the door. A firm voice emerged from the room, "Yes, who is it?"

I replied, "Sir, its Satyam. May I come in please?"

"Yes, come in" said the Headmaster.

When I opened the door, I noticed that the Headmaster sir was scrutinizing few papers. Might be my bio data, I guessed.

I wished him and he nodded in response. He continued with his scrutiny while I took a quick look around. The room was quite big and well furnished. The Headmaster's table had a bulky vintage look. It was placed in the centre of room with a huge window located behind it. All the almirahs were on the left side of the room. One pen stand, a globe and an ashtray along with some report cards and few files were placed very neatly on the table.

Headmaster looked at me and asked in a firm voice, "How are you young man?

For a moment, I was not able to utter a word. I babbled but somehow managed to reply, "I.......I am fine sir, th......thank you for asking, sir."

He glanced at his watch and said while scribbling something on a piece of paper."Very well... you are quite punctual".

He continued, "I have seen your records from the previous school and the result of the test conducted this afternoon. Hope you will keep up with your performance."

I replied, "Sir, yes sir....I will do my best." Finally, I said something audible and that too without babbling.

The Headmaster pressed the office bell to call the peon but no one answered.

The next bell was accompanied by an announcement in soft and gentle voice, "Please fasten your seatbelts; we are about to land".This was the airplane addressing system which woke me up from the state of nostalgia.

I adjusted my seat to the upright position and fastened my seat belt. I looked at Shreya; she was busy jotting down something in her diary.

I asked while placing the magazine back in the seat pocket, "What are you writing?"

Shreya replied, "Just making a to-do list."

After having done with the list, she closed her diary and said while placing it in her hand bag, "Going to land. Holidays are over now". She smiled and fastened her seatbelt.

Chapter-2

Don't let emotions overpower your decisions

Our flight landed at the Delhi airport. After completing all the formalities we collected our luggage and hired a taxi to our residence. While on our way to home, Shreya's mobile phone started ringing. Like always, she searched her entire bag before locating the pocket where she had kept her mobile. Sometimes, I wonder whether is she aware or not of all the contents of her purse which she carries all day long on her shoulder. It was better for me to leave this topic because advising her is an open invitation to a never ending argument.

Shreya finally got hold of her mobile phone and attended to the call "Hi Sandhya, how are you? Well, we just returned from................" She paused and did not utter a word but kept listening.

After listening to her cousin, she replied with a grave expression. "I will call you back, bye".

I asked inquisitively, "What happened? Is everything alright?"

"We'll talk about it later" Shreya replied in a serious tone. (Within an hour we reached our home.)

After unlocking the main door, we stepped inside the home. I drew the curtains apart in the drawing room while Shreya seated herself on the sofa. "So what was the phone call about?" I asked as I turned towards her.

Shreya replied with a grief filled voice, "R.P. Uncle passed away last night..."

R.P. Uncle was a distant relative of Shreya; he was also a fatherly figure for her and a mentor. He had a very jolly nature and often used to say that people will miss him when he is gone. My God, he was right. I was wondering how unpredictable the life is and at the same time, I was also thinking about the pending work at my office and my possible meeting with an overseas client.

I understand relations are an important part of life but career and financial growth are also among the top priorities in life. We need money to sustain our self, our relations and almost everything around.

"What should I tell Sandhya? What should we do? Will we be able to manage to visit Shimla in such a short notice?" asked Shreya while wiping the tears from her cheeks.

"It will be difficult but attending to his last rites is also equally important. We can't shun our responsibilities in the name of business" I replied thoughtfully.

Shreya was surprised on hearing this as I seldom talk about human values and relations.

I paused a little and said while looking at her, "I will manage but what about you. Will you be able to skip hospital for few more days?"

Shreya replied, "It would be difficult; will try."

She took out her mobile phone and informed the hospital administration regarding extension of her leave by few more days due to sudden demise of her uncle.

"You should freshen up and pack for our journey to Shimla. Till then, I will check on my office mails and other important stuff" I told her while opening my laptop.

I started going through my emails and business updates on my laptop. Meanwhile, my secretary called up on my cell phone and reminded me about the appointment with foreign clients on coming Saturday. This left me with only two days in hand to reach back to Delhi from Shimla.

Unlike most of the girls, Shreya was quick under the shower.

In a while, she was dressed up and combing her hair. By then, I had already checked my mails and made the necessary phone calls.

Shreya had overheard a part of my conversation with my secretary and was inquiring about it but that was not the right time to discuss it with her. So, I left it for later.

Instead, I said while switching off my cell phone and laptop, "I shall also freshen up".

Shreya got up from her dressing table and said while moving towards the kitchen, "I will prepare breakfast and some snacks to carry along with us. You get ready quickly".

We packed our stuff, had breakfast and were ready to start our journey. Although, I was tired but the feeling of visiting my homeland Shimla always filled me up with enthusiasm.

I took the luggage and kept it in the boot space of our car. Shreya like always ensured that everything inside the house is in proper place. She checked the switches, locked the house and informed our neighbors about our travel.

I asked while turning the ignition on, "Why do you always have to inform the neighbours before leaving. I mean, who does all this stuff nowadays?"

She replied while wearing the seatbelt, "It's important to en-sure safety of one's house."

With this little note, we finally started with our journey to Shimla. It was more of a silent journey. After travelling for about five hours as we approached the hilly terrains, we got mesmerized by the serenity and beauty of the nature; so both of us were lost in our own thoughts.

The mountains transcend you to an elated state of mind and soul. Here everything appears to be serene, calm and peaceful; simply divine. Decked with rich vegetation in lower ranges and with snow on the higher ranges, they play a key role in sustain-ing life.

I broke the silence as I said while rolling down the window, "Hills and the vicinity are appearing to be different from the way I remember them. With much wider roads and new de-veloping satellite townships in otherwise dense forest areas, things have changed in here."

"It's good to see the development" Shreya replied while gazing through the window,

"Yeah" I said.

Suddenly, Shreya exclaimed, "Look....look...a toy train (trains which ply on narrow gauge railway lines) I adore them since my childhood."

I smiled at her and replied, "Yes, they are amazing".

I pulled over to enjoy the scenic beauty augmented by this wonderful piece of architecture. We enjoyed that moment and also had a light hearted conversation. I don't remember the last time we interacted like this. The only things that come to my mind nowadays are pay checks and clients orders.

With a fresh mind and enriched emotions, we continued further with our journey. On the very next curve, the first thing which caught our attention was a signboard placed at the intersection. The board read, "The Convent of Hills, The School with a difference".

Shreya spoke up after reading the board, "Satyam, if I am not wrong, this is the school where you studied."

I smiled while nodding but said nothing; this sight unleashed a rally of memories running in front of my eyes.

I found myself standing in the Headmaster's room where he was repeatedly ringing the bell to call in the peon. On the third bell, peon entered in the room. He took the paper from the hands of Head-master and left.

During the interaction with him, I did not notice any change of expressions on his face.

After the peon left, the Headmaster opened a file and started reading it. I was sitting clueless waiting for further questions or instructions from him. However, he did not speak a word but kept reading his file.

After a while, somebody knocked at the door. I tried looking towards the door from the corner of my eye and could make out that two people were standing at the doorstep.

Headmaster looked at me and said, "Satyam, you must be aware of the fact that this school is a residential school. I would like to introduce you to your roommate. He's a very brilliant student and the captain of our sports team. "

The Headmaster introduced me to the boy, the one whom I had just met in the corridor and said, "Satyam, he is Kartik, your roommate". I think both of you can leave now.

Both of us wished the Headmaster and left the room.

I said, "So, you will be my roommate for next three years; good to meet you again."

Kartik smiled and asked, "How was the test?"

I replied, "It was good, but the Headmaster sir appears to be a bit strange."

"He is a tough task master but believe me he is a great teacher and mentor. You will gradually get to know him" Kartik said.

Kartik led me to our room no. 108 on the first floor. The room was spacious with ample sunlight and cross ventilation. Kartik opened the lock and said before leaving, "Satyam, I think you must be hungry. So freshen up and come downstairs to the canteen. I will meet you there".

"Alright, I will be there" I replied.

I was happy as I was feeling confident for the first time in my life. After placing my bag in the room, I quickly walked towards the parking area to share the details of admission with my parents.

Both of them were waiting eagerly to know the final result and were elated to hear that I had successfully secured a place in the school. They wished me luck and left.

On my way back to the hostel, initially, I thought about unpacking my stuff but I was really hungry. Therefore, I decided to go to the canteen first and leave the unpacking for later.

I paced my way towards the canteen but was disappointed to read the board hanging on the canteen door stating 'next meal to be served after 7pm'. There was no point in entering the canteen; therefore I started walking towards my room in despair and with a hope of finding an eatable packed in my luggage.

On my way back, I was trying to figure out why Kartik might have called me to the canteen when they are not serving. Perhaps, I assumed that this must be his idea to rag me with his friends. For a moment, I got frightened but then I regained my poise and decided to face the fear. Instead of running away, I walked straight towards the canteen.

I opened the door only to find an empty canteen except for the housekeeping staff. Then unexpectedly, somebody patted on my shoulder. I turned around to find Kartik holding a tray with a burger and a bottle of cold drink on it.

He said while handing over the tray to me, "Where were you? I presumed that you might be taking rest. Well, the burger is not that hot but still consumable."

I thanked him wholeheartedly for the kind gesture. There was nobody else with him to rag me. It was nothing more than an illusion and a fear worth overcoming.

I accepted the tray being a bit reluctant and asked him, "From where did you manage all this stuff..... Canteen is closed and counters will reopen only at 7pm".

I continued while biting on to the burger, "It appears that you share a good rapport with people around in here."

Kartik, unmoved by appreciation replied in a modest way, "No....the canteen staff is quite generous and co-operative."

"Satyam, I think we should take a break." Shreya said interrupting my chain of thoughts.

I regained my orientation and pulled over in front of a café. We stepped out of the car to have a cup of coffee. We seated ourselves at a table meant for two people nearby a centrally located fountain. Shreya spoke up, "I still can't believe that uncle is no more. The last time when I met him, he was in pink of health. He always stood by my side, kept motivating me and helped me in achieving my ambition."

I said assuring her, "The pain of losing or parting with someone whom you regard or love is intense, indeed. I understand it because I also had to say goodbye to my best friend forever and unfortunately we never met again. Such losses leave a void in heart. Initially, it is hard to cope-up with the loss but life keeps on moving."

"What happened to him?" she asked.

I replied while placing the coffee mug on the table, "He had to leave the school, the one that you noticed on the way; in the mid-session to shoulder his family responsibilities after sudden demise of his father."

I continued while taking out my wallet to pay the bill, "I miss him the most because he was the only one who was true to me as a friend. However, life stops for no one. It keeps on going at its own pace."

Shreya replied, "This is how life is. Isn't it? Still the loss of our dear ones pains us and emotions often overpower our minds for a while."

By that time Shreya had also finished her coffee. We paid the bill and resumed our journey.

After travelling for another 45 minutes, we reached her uncle's house. The scenario around was indeed depressing and appeared quite scary to me. People were sitting in groups and with arrival of every relative the ladies present would start weeping inconsolably. Shreya's cousin came running towards her and hugged her firmly. Both of them started crying and were simultaneously trying to console each other.

I was standing confused and must be appearing like a statue to others but what else could I do? No matter how wise you are; under these circumstances, it is not unusual to go blank.

I was only physically present there; my mind was continuously engaged in planning the upcoming meeting with my investors.

By evening, I had sorted out everything about my most awaited meeting with an overseas client and was eager to go back to Delhi and strike the scheduled business deal.

Now I was faced with a very complicated situation and that was - to convince Shreya to return to Delhi next morning.

I was dubious about this idea as she might consider me as a heartless or a money-minded person and it would further tarnish my already dented image. She might even think me of as a sham because the human values which I was preaching before the onset of our journey to Shimla may not be reflected well in my decision to return immediately and that too for a business meeting. I was in a fix because if I failed to reach back on time, I would have lost millions.

After a bit of brain storming, I finally decided that it is better to get labeled as a heartless instead of losing on such a big fortune.

In the night, I told Shreya about the business meeting for which we were supposed to leave for Delhi in the morning. Contrary to what I had expected, she approved of my plan without questioning.

Next morning when we were about to start our journey back to Delhi, Shreya insisted after seating herself in the car, "I think we must pay a short visit at our family home to meet Mom and Dad."

I said while putting on the seat belt, "I have already told you about my meeting scheduled for tomorrow morning."

I continued assuring, "I don't think we can meet them today but I promise once the project is finalized, we will revisit Shimla."

Shreya replied thoughtfully and said with great concern, "Satyam, how can we leave without meeting Mom and Dad, especially after coming this far? I don't think this is a fair decision."

Initially, I tried not to answer her in the heat of the moment as it could result in an unrequired argument which I always preferred to avoid.

After thinking calmly for a while, I replied, "Okay, we'll go but only for few hours. I cannot afford to miss my appointment".

"Come on, let's surprise them" Shreya said cheerfully.

I started driving towards our home in Shimla. Although, I did not speak to her but I appreciated her concern and respect for my parents.

After about an hour's drive, we reached our family home. It was a lovely mansion, harboring innumerous memories from my childhood. Everything around looked the same as it was in the good old days. We entered the drive way and drove towards the garage. I parked the car next to the vintage Cadillac parked in the garage. It was my father's first car and he has managed to maintain it in the running condition even till now.

I was about to meet them after a considerable period of time. I think it's understandable to find it difficult to spare time for your personal commitments when you start with a new business venture because you need to dedicate the majority of your time to it. Success doesn't come cheap.

Mother answered the door and she was delighted to see us. We greeted her and had a little hearty conversation while standing at the doorstep. Thereafter we stepped inside and I asked her while walking towards the living room, "Where is father? Is he not around".

"He's in the garden, I will call him" mother replied.

"Wait mom, I will love to surprise him" I said as I moved towards the garden,

I walked swiftly towards the garden where dad was adding manure around the roots of newly planted rose shrubs. As he looked at me, his face lightened up. He quickly got up and said while hugging me, "How are you my dear? This is a very pleasant surprise."

He took out his gardening gloves and said while sitting on a chair in the garden, "How is your business doing? It must be good."

"Yeah, its fine" I replied thoughtfully while pulling a chair for myself.

He said, "Your mother had told me few days back that you are starting with a new software firm. Is it so? However, this indeed appears to be a very futuristic decision."

I said confidently, "In fact, tomorrow morning I am having a meeting with an overseas client for this new venture."

"That's good" he replied.

I was happy by the manner in which my father appreciated my success. This always acts as a motivation for me to do more and more.

I poured juice into two glasses from the tetra pack brought by Shreya on a serving tray, handed over a glass to my father and asked, "So, how is everything going here?"

Father took few sips and said after placing the glass back on the table, "Well, your mother and I are now enjoying a retired life."

I asked astonishingly, "What about the business? Who looks after it?"

"It's going as usual" father replied.

"But you just said that you are now enjoying retired life?" I asked.

Father replied, "Over the years, I have not only developed various business ventures but have also developed a pool of dedicated and trusted human assets. This retired life has been made possible because of them."

I was listening keenly as I was curious to know that how could anyone rely on his staff for running his business.

Looking at my curiosity, he smiled a little and said, "I know what you are thinking about but some things cannot be taught instantly; you learn them with time as you get more experienced. However, always remember that if you have recruited the appropriate type of employees and you trust their abilities at work, then your company would definitely reach the heights of progress."

What type of an employee is appropriate to be hired?" I asked.

Father said, "You will get this over a period of time as with experience you will be able to understand the human psychology and human behaviors much better which will in turn help you in identifying and hiring the right set of employees based on their working techniques and task management skills."

Our conversation was interrupted by the call for lunch from mom. He got up from the chair and continued, "Come son; we should move now. We'll discuss this later."

After the lunch and a short but cheerful get-together, we continued with our journey back to Delhi. We had spent only an hour with them but they were quite happy to see us after a gap of one year. It was a heart-warming visit.

I was happy that Shreya had insisted and convinced me to meet them. If we had left without meeting them, they would have definitely felt bad about it.

"Shreya, you are quite good in keeping up with relationships. Thanks for making this lovely moment to happen today" I said while wearing the seat belt.

She smiled and held on to my hand firmly but said nothing.

Sometimes actions speak for themselves and often louder than what words could have confessed.

Chapter-3

Never lose touch with humanity

An incomprehensible voice was coming from some-where; it appeared as if somebody was calling out. I tried hard listening to it but could not make out anything clearly. It may be due to the pillow which might have tumbled upon my head. Gradually the voice grew clearer and louder. It was Shreya yelling from the kitchen, "Wake up Satyam, it is already 7 am. What about your urgent meeting? Wake up dear."

Startled, I sat upright and checked the table clock after flinging the pillow aside. It was ten past seven. I could hear the ringing sound of toaster from the kitchen. I got up hurriedly and rushed into the bathroom to freshen up. Meanwhile, Shreya was busy preparing breakfast in the kitchen. By 7.45 a.m. breakfast was ready and so was I.

Shreya said while serving breakfast, "Don't you have an important meeting today?"

"Thanks for waking me up. I was so tired that I must have forgotten to set an alarm for the morning."I replied while taking a slice of bread from the serving plate and applying butter on it

I placed the butter knife back on the tray and continued, "I can drop you at your hospital today but please don't take too long to get ready."

Shreya turned the two inverted glasses in the upright position on the dining table and replied while pouring milk in them, "I will be quick. I have an operation scheduled at 9, so even I can't afford to be late today."

Shreya continued, "Even slightest of negligence can lead to serious repercussions and that is not at all acceptable to me. Moreover, my H.O.D will also get a topic to embarrass me, if I am late today."

We hurriedly had our breakfast and in the next few minutes, we were heading in our car towards my office. Shreya's hospital was en-route; therefore, dropping her was never an issue.

Even after extensive brainstorming and homework, the previous meeting with an investor was unfruitful. Therefore, I was a bit apprehensive about this upcoming meeting as the stakes were high this time.

Shreya turned towards me and asked, "You look so worried and thoughtful. Is everything alright?"

I replied while looking at the side mirror, "Little nervous about the meeting. If everything goes as per the plan, it will provide a big boost to our newly started software company."

Shreya opened her handbag, looked for something in it and said after closing the bag, "Don't worry things will go in your favor. I don't understand the need of floating a new company this early as you are already into automobile parts and hardware business. Don't you think expansion at this stage might be taxing and there are chances that things may go haywire?"

We were stopped at a red light, I looked at her and said, "Software is the future and it is always better to stay ahead. I can handle all of this; trust me. You were telling something about an operation scheduled for today."

"Don't know about the case or patient. In the morning, I received a text message from my colleague that I have been included in the team of doctors" she replied.

By that time the traffic light had turned green. I asked while speeding the vehicle, "Who is going to operate?"

Shreya replied bleakly, "The H.O.D."

I asked inquisitively, "So why are you afraid of assisting your

H.O.D. in the operation theater."

She replied irritatingly, "To understand that you have to be a medical student."

"No, I think one must understand all the concepts and procedures meticulously, then it doesn't matter whether you are assisting the H.O.D. or performing the procedure alone" I said while smiling.

Shreya replied candidly, "Thanks for such a lovely advice. I never knew husbands can be so smart and sound this wise too."

I said while slowing down the car, "Even I don't understand that how does a woman acquire all the knowledge and experience in eternity as soon as she becomes a wife and the man loses all of it."

Shreya giggled and said, "Thanks for alleviating my mood."

I said while pulling over the vehicle, "Here is your destination, doctor."

Shreya quickly gave a gentle peck on my cheek, opened the car's door and waved me goodbye before rushing inside the hospital.

I waved back at her and left towards my office. My mind was once again embroiled with the thoughts of upcoming meeting.

Just to make things simple, I called up my secretary using the Bluetooth device.

The call was answered in the first bell, "Good morning sir"

I said hurriedly, "Ishika, I am on my way to the office. Keep all the relevant documents for the meeting ready on my table."

I disconnected the call without waiting for her reply.

Usually, I reach office around 11:00 am but today I reached at 9:45 am. I knew that it was going to be a surprise to my office staff, perhaps a very unpleasant one. When I entered the office, attentiveness and enthusiasm were altogether absent in the staff. From the security guard to the lift boy and from the peon to the programmers; the entire staff was behaving in a manner as if instead of in an office they are loitering in a shopping complex.

The first person to notice me was a newly hired programmer. He reacted in a manner as if he had seen a ghost. All of a sudden, the basking employees were fully charged up. In a blink of an eye, the entire staff was seated in their respective positions and every one was pretending to look busy with their computers or documents, whatever they could get hold of. Even the peon was scrutinizing the pocket calendar as if he was examining a CT scan report.

Such chaotic behavior of the staff angered me. Controlling my anger, I paced swiftly towards my room ignoring the salute given by the peon.

I entered my room while reading some messages on my phone. I removed my coat, placed it on the coat hanger and walked towards my table to take a look at the documents for the upcoming meeting.

I placed the mobile phone on the table and was enraged to find a completely empty table. I quickly called up my secretary on the intercom but she was unavailable.

Her assistant informed me that she has gone to collect documents from the photocopy section and will be in my cabin in few minutes. Finding it inappropriate to express my annoyance to her, I disconnected the phone call immediately.

I was supposed to attend the meeting in next 45 minutes and that too without any preparations at all. This was scary but years ago, I had volunteered myself to do something very much similar.

One day after a class test, our class teacher asked Kartik and me to carry the test notebooks to the staffroom.

We both got up from our seats and walked towards his table to pick up the notebooks. Although I had picked up the shorter pile, still it was tall enough to obscure my vision. I had to constantly keep my neck tilted to one side to be able to traverse my way to the staffroom. On the other hand, may be due to his taller stature, Kartik appeared to carry the notebooks comfortably.

On our way towards the staffroom, he stopped by the school notice board and said after reading it, "Satyam, I think you should also take a look."

I answered annoyingly as I was eager to get rid of that pile of the notebooks, "Are they going to pull this down. Can't we see it later?"

Kartik said while running his finger over the glass shield of the notice board, "Oh come on, it will just take a second." He looked towards me and continued, "I can take few of the notebooks if you wish to."

I replied reluctantly while moving towards the notice board, "It's all right, I can carry them."

I read the notice; it was regarding a debate competition and the most challenging part was that the topics were to be allotted only half an hour before the actual event.

"This will be fun. I think we should participate in this. What do you say Satyam?" Kartik spoke enthusiastically as we started walking towards the staffroom which was a few meters away from the notice board.

I replied while tilting my neck to the right so that I could have a much better view of the path I was walking, "Let me think about it. I can always think better with my neck straight."

"Oh sure" Kartik replied while controlling his laugh as we were just about to enter the staffroom.

We wished the teachers present in the staffroom, kept the notebooks on the teacher's desk and walked out quickly to avoid another possible task by some other teacher.

To decide about participating in that debate was indeed a tough call as it was beyond my capabilities. Moreover, I did not want to ruin my recently established reputation in the new school by refusing to participate.

I had a profound stage fear. I find it quite difficult to deliver even for the topics that are rehearsed hundreds of times. So, to perform without preparation was beyond my imagination. Once I climb-up the stage, I cannot see anything except the microphone and hear a sound except for my mumbling. I get frozen, every time I climb up on the stage.

I started to think of an excuse with which I could easily escape the situation but nothing substantive was coming in my mind.

While I was jostling with my mind, Kartik asked me, "So, what has the man with straight neck decided now?"

"Yes...yes we must participate. Debates are an innovative way to expand one's knowledge." I replied while controlling my anxiety.

Kartik looked towards me and said, "Good, let's give our names for the competition."

I said, "I don't know that how will I perform without any preparation."

"You will be just fine.Trust me;just climb up that stage and speak up your mind." He said.

Kartik continued as we walked towards the classroom, "I have participated in this kind of competition earlier and it is not unusual for the students to go blank on the stage. After all, it is not easy to deliver without preparation".

After a lot of brainstorming, I finally made up my mind to participate in that event.

The day of debate arrived. All the participants were called in the auditorium and topics were allotted to us.

Coincidently, both of us got the same topic 'Importance of relationships in the present society'. Two groups were formed; first group was to speak for the topic and second group was to speak against the topic. I was in the second group, whereas, Kartik was in the first one.

All the students marched towards the backstage to jot down the relevant points to present them in a much organized and logical manner on the stage.

I also took out my pen and started jotting down important points for the debate on a notebook, which I was carrying along with me.

After writing down all the relevant points that were coming to my mind, I detached the sheet from the notebook and placed it in my blazer's pocket. I then glanced at Kartik's notepad and to my amusement I could only see concentric circles drawn on it.

I asked him, "Aren't you preparing for the debate?"

He smiled and said, "I have already done with my preparation".

Before I could ask him any further, an announcement was made over the classroom addressing system requesting all the partici-

pants to walk into the auditorium and get seated at the designated places.

I was the third speaker from my side. A student from Class-XII opened the debate from our side and his points were very wisely countered by the other team. No doubt that the quality of the content expressed by the participants and the level of patience exhibited by the audience was remarkable.

When my name was called, I became nervous for a moment. I was not sure whether my views will appear mature enough to the audience or I will be mocked for expressing them. However, I convinced myself that this is a now or never situation. If I would not stand for my views today, then how am I going to stand for what I believe in for the rest of my life?

Therefore, I stepped on the stage leaving behind all my worries and fears.

I greeted every one and started with my speech:

"My name is Satyam Sharma. The topic for today's discussion is-'Importance of relationships in the present society' and I am speaking against the topic.

Speaking against the topic does not imply that I don't like friends or don't believe in family structure. However, what I have observed around me is somewhat different and certainly my observations might not go in favour of relationships.

Over a period of time everything around us has changed and evolved. Change is the only constant thing which we witness throughout our lives. I am not against changes; they are good and we need them to evolve and grow. Similarly our perception towards our relationships has also changed significantly over a period of time. It appears to me as if more and more people are losing personal touch and concern for their fellows.

In most of the households that I have seen, siblings fight with each other and parents act like a match referee who do their best to stop the ongoing fights. Once they grow up, they almost completely forget each other. They meet either in funerals or in weddings. They also meet with an intention to snatch shares from each other when an advocate pronounces their father's will.

Nothing stays forever in this world. We live, we die, we earn and we lose. Man is not immune to ageing and neither are the memories.

Money is of utmost importance nowadays and our lives revolve around profits and comforts. Most of us have left no respect, love or patience for our relationships.

A person who supported us in our bad times, who fought and sacrificed selflessly for us, loses importance with time. Concept of gratitude is obsolete now as we believe in opportunism. Person who still believes in commitments is considered to be foolish, possessive and interfering.

Our ageing parents become a burden, siblings become rivals and sometimes spouse becomes a nagging element. There are certain unanswered questions which keep creeping inside my mind, like:

Why ingratitude and meanness has plagued our society?

Why saints lead a bitter life and die painfully?

Why brothers become botherations?

Why people do not hesitate to cheat a person who sacrificed his/her entire life for them?

We all have heard and seen many stories of cheating, back- stabbing and family hostility. When all such nuisance is prevailing in society, then how can I say that relationships in the present society are gold and not phony?

> *Thank you all."*

There was a pin drop silence in the hall which was broken by a round of applause. I heaved a sigh of relief after completing my speech. For first time in my life, I had successfully faced and con-

quered the worst fear of my life, i.e. stage fear. I was already feeling like a winner.

As I stepped down, the coordinator climbed up the stage and said, "Very well, atmosphere is getting warmed up. Satyam has expressed very intensive, intrusive and well-articulated facts from which we cannot hide ourselves. Now let us see, what the next contestant has to deliver. The next contestant is Kartik from Tagore house."

The entire hall was resonating with the sounds of clapping and cheers. The intensity of the applause could very well reflect the level of Kartik's popularity in the school.

I was also keen to listen to him. Not because he was a popular student or my friend but I wanted to know how well could he perform by simply drawing concentric circles in his notebook.

Kartik stepped in holding the mike in his hands and spoke: "Respected teachers and dear friends. You all must have paid attention to what my dear friend Satyam just shared with all of us.

I was listening to him very carefully and indeed he made some very valid points. I agree with most of them. However, I will still speak for the topic.

Dear friends, I want to understand why do we always seek reci-

procity in relationships? Why do we judge people by their words and not by their acts? Why don't we show patience towards our relationships? After-all, it is the family and friends whom we look upon in the hour of need.

I have witnessed this very common yet strange behavior that we do our best to tolerate bad words or bullying by people surrounding us; be it your neighbour, classmate or any other socially related member. In fact, we present best of our demeanors and even try to cool off the situations in public. However, we act very differently when we are at home, especially in the company of our parents, siblings or spouse. All of a sudden, some drastic transformations occur in our behaviour and then we are not able to tolerate even a slightest increase in the pitch of voice of our family member. A simple logical remark made by our parents or spouse towards our noted behaviour or action appears to be disrespectful, demeaning and highly objectionable to us.

We argue, quarrel and say a lot of unrequired and useless stuff.

Have you ever thought how deeply we hurt people who love us immensely and selflessly? What happens to our convent education and mannerism under those circumstances?

The fact is that we are losing our touch with the humanity. That is why we abide under fear and repel otherwise.

If this is not true then tell me, what makes us to tolerate scolding by a teacher or a boss but cannot stand a single word spoken by our father? Reason is simple; we listen to our boss as we have fear of losing our job and to our teacher as we fear failing but no such fear is associated with our family members. That is why they appear to be irritating and unworthy.

Our acts are always guided by our own judgments, perceptions and experience but we still want the other person to act according to our whims.

Interestingly, we always like to guide family and friends on various issues. We insist them to deal a particular situation as per our advice but when somebody attempts to guide us to do a work in a certain way; we label that person as interfering.

Why can't we simply love and respect instead of quarreling and badmouthing.

Today, I am going to try my best to convince you and my dear friend Satyam to accept the fact that, 'Relationships and emotions are the real treasure of human life' and"...
...............*Before he could complete his statement, an announcement was done via class room addressing system. The announcement was followed by prominent knocking sounds. It appeared as if*

somebody was knocking repeatedly at the door.

Chapter-4

Always maintain your self esteem

A voice accompanied the knocking. I could clearly hear; it was Ishika, my secretary who was seeking permission to come in.

I said while looking towards the door, "Please come in."

She wished me promptly while opening the door, "Good morning sir".

I ignored her greeting and asked in a very firm tone, "Ishika, I think I had called you half an hour ago?"

"Yes sir, I had received your call" she replied.

I asked her, "Did you hear me properly then?"

"Yes sir, I had heard you properly" she replied anxiously.

"In that case would you like to explain this or are you also finding it difficult to keep up with the pace and requirements of the job like others?" I asked angrily while turning my gaze towards the empty table.

I could see her getting teary eyed and I dislike such display of emotions at work place. People don't discharge their duties properly and when asked, they start exhibiting plethora of emotions to cover for their inefficiency.

We all are here for some serious work. The same work which keeps us going and helps us to earn money for our families. In order to execute that work we need to comply with our duties and responsibilities which people fail to do.

I asked her with a restrained tone, "Ishika, would you like to elaborate why are we not prepared for the 11 a. m. meeting? What am I supposed to do in the meeting; serve coffee to the clients?"

She replied hesitantly, "Sir, I had completed all the paper work last evening."

"Then show me" I said.

She mustered up some courage and replied calmly, "Sir, I had handed over the documents to one of the interns and she was supposed to make three copies each of the documents, bind them neatly and place them at your table by 9:30 this morning."

"Then where are the documents? Why did she not comply with your instruction?" I said angrily while glancing at my watch.

Ishika replied with an expression of irritation, "Sir I tried calling her multiple times since morning but…"

"But she is not answering to your calls. Fire her right away. (I walked towards my chair and said) She might be doing internship here but you are not. Where is your backup?" I spoke scornfully.

I took out a pen drive from my pocket and continued, "One more thing, I have noticed that the performance of Nikita is declining continuously and I don't think we can utilize her in our office. Therefore, I am terminating her services. You should inform her and complete the necessary paper work in this matter."

I switched on my laptop and said while inserting the pen drive in the laptop, "We still have half an hour for the meeting. Bring me the details; I will prepare something worth presenting. Also, send me a cup of hot coffee if that is not too much to ask for?"

She quickly walked out of my office. From the glass door, I could easily see her soliloquizing on her way to her cubicle.

I turned my attention towards the saved files on my pen drive and after studying the old documents which I had kept in my table's drawer, I prepared a detailed presentation regarding execution of the project on my computer. I was able to finish it up within those thirty minutes before the arrival of the investors and was having something worth presenting with me.

The meeting went well. I was able to convince the investors and clients that they will be benefited by investing in my project. Except for few initial doubts and a lengthy discussion on one topic, everything went smooth and finally I was able to sign the most awaited contract.

I called up Shreya to share this news with her.

She answered my call in a very dull tone, "Hello Satyam, how are you? Tell me what is it?"

"What happened? Why are you sounding so low? Is everything all right?" I asked her anxiously.

"Yes everything is fine here. How was your meeting?" she tried to speak calmly.

Sensing her uneasiness, I did not probe any further and said, "The meeting was good and our company has successfully signed the contract. I will be leaving for the home in an hour. What about you?"

She replied, "I am really happy for you. Listen I will have to rush now, the senior doctor is calling me."

I could overhear someone calling her urgently to the ICU.

Shreya disconnected the call and headed towards the ICU. She was startled by looking at the number of people gathered at the ICU door.

She asked the nurse who had come to call her, "What happened sister Neeta; why are so many people gathered here?"

The nurse was clueless and answered, "Everything was fine when I had come to call you....."

"Let us check the patient quickly" Shreya replied instantly.

As they made their way into the unit, Shreya requested the attendants, "Please avoid overcrowding here, only one person may stay but the rest will have to leave."

The nurse ensured that the instructions were complied with.

Shreya checked the monitor and was relieved to see normal readings of the vital signs of the patient who was under resuscitation.

Shreya pulled a stool and sat next to the patient. She checked the vitals periodically and noted them down on the patient chart. After an hour, the nurse came walking swiftly in the unit and informed that the H.O.D. is on his way to examine the patient.

Shreya immediately got up and said to the nurse, "I hope he doesn't behave pernickety today."

"Hope so" she replied.

"I don't know why he is always in such a bad mood" Shreya said.

Before she could speak another word the H.O.D. entered the ICU. They both looked nervously at each other. God forbid what if he had overheard their conversation. They were skeptical until he started examining the patient which implied that he had heard nothing. Shreya and Neeta both felt relieved.

He checked the patient and said, "His condition is stable and improving. We can shift him to the special ward now."

"Yes Sir" both of them replied in unison.

Listening to this univocal reply, he looked suspiciously at them and asked, "Who will be on night duty today?"

Shreya looked at Neeta and replied, "The duty roster is not out yet. However, I am attending to the patient since this morning."

"First, shift the patient to the ward, then we will talk over this matter later" he said as he moved out of the I.C.U.

The relatives were informed and the patient was shifted to the special ward.

After the patient was shifted to special ward, the H.O.D. examined him again and said to his attendant while prescribing medicines on the case sheet, "He has recovered up to a considerable extent. These are the medicines which are to be given from today evening onwards. You can also bring fresh fruit juice for him now."

As the attendant left the special ward, the H.O.D. turned towards Shreya and Neeta and asked firmly, "Where is the duty roster?"

Neeta replied, "Sir, the duty roster was sent twice to your office but it was returned unsigned. So……..Dr. Shreya is attending to the patient…..since this morning."

He replied irritably, "Ok then, this must be my mistake."

"I didn't mean that, Sir" Neeta replied promptly.

Neeta opened a file which she was carrying along with her and said while handing over it to the H.O.D., "Sir here is the roster; it was prepared by Dr. Aditya in the morning."

The H.O.D. looked at the roster, made a few changes and signed it. He returned it to Neeta and said before leaving, "Here you go. No room for any confusion anymore."

Meanwhile, the attendant had returned from the pharmacy.

Shreya told him, "In case you need to consult, you can call at the doctor's duty room at extension no. 20."

Neeta and Shreya both walked out of the ward to the duty room. Upon reaching the room, Neeta said, "I think I should pin it up on the notice board."

She took out the paper from the file and gave a surprised look to Shreya after reading it.

"What happened?" Shreya asked while taking the paper from Neeta.

Shreya said irritatingly after looking at the roster, "What? How can he do that? I have already completed my shift and he has put me on duty till the midnight."

"Why don't you go and talk to him?" Neeta asked.

Shreya replied, "It's already 8 p.m. Instead of talking to him, I would prefer to leave the hospital at around 12 a.m. How am I going to appear tomorrow for the morning shift? I don't know why is he so rude? I wonder from where he derives so much energy to stay angry throughout the day."

Shreya sat on the chair and continued, "Fine. I'll try my best. I think, I should inform Satyam about this mistimed shift."

Neeta smiled and said while looking out of the window, "Are you going to ask him to pick you up from the hospital?"

"No, we have just returned from a very long and tiring trip. He was also having an important meeting today; he must be tired. I will hire a cab back home." Shreya replied as she took out her mobile phone from her bag.

Neeta added further, "You appear to be a very concerned wife."

Shreya smiled and signaled Neeta to stay quiet as the call had connected.

Shreya said, "Hello, Satyam"

"Where are you? I was waiting for your call" I replied.

Shreya said, "Sorry dear, I am stuck at work."

"Oh; anything serious?" I asked.

"No….no….nothing like that, just a routine case but my H.O.D. has put me on duty till the midnight" Shreya replied.

"Look, no one wants to leave you" I joked.

Shreya took a deep breath and replied, "May be, what can be done."

"Have you had your meal?" I asked.

"Not yet, but we'll have something in a while" Shreya replied.

I asked, "Would you like to have a pizza?"

"I think you should have dinner and take some rest at home. I will hire a cab instead" Shreya replied while trying to conclude the call as Neeta was also listening to their conversation.

I said, "I am still waiting for your answer."

Shreya glanced at Neeta who was constantly looking at her and was smiling while listening to her conversation. So she said in a bleak voice, "I am not alone, people are listening. Can we talk later?"

"Ok….ok…ok…..one last question" I said hurriedly.

"What is it Satyam?" Shreya asked promptly.

"Can you please come up to the window?" I replied.

Neeta was already standing near window. Shreya stood up, walked towards the window and was surprised to see Satyam standing next to his black SUV in the parking; holding a casket of Pizza in his hand. He signaled her to come down.

Shreya looked at Neeta. Neeta chuckled and said, "You must go. In case of any emergency, I will call you immediately."

Shreya happily dashed her way to the parking where Satyam was waiting for her and said to him, "What a pleasant surprise. I never expected this? When did you arrive?"

I said while handing over the casket, "First have some food, it is fresh and hot. You must be hungry."

Shreya said while taking the box from Satyam, "Thanks for bringing this".

"When and why did you come?" she asked

I replied, "You appeared a little stressed out when I had called you from the office. Therefore, instead of waiting for you at home, I decided to come here to pick you up."

"Alright but I will be free by midnight. What will you do till then?" Shreya asked.

I said while glancing at my watch, "It is almost 8:30 p.m. I will watch a movie or do some work on my laptop; you don't worry for me."

I continued while pointing towards the window where Neeta stood by scrolling her mobile phone, "Look your friend is waiting for you, go and have your meal. It is still consumable."

Shreya went back cheerfully and waved at me from the window after reaching her duty room. I waved back at her and opened the door of my car to get inside. While working on my laptop, I could clearly hear the announcements being made over the addressing system of the hospital calling for one doctor or another.

I was feeling a little drowsy, so I locked my car and rolled the windows down a little for cross ventilation. The announcements were still audible but were gradually becoming incomprehensible.

I could clearly hear the announcement which had interrupted Kartik's speech during the debate.

"Kartik and Satyam are requested to report to the Headmaster's room immediately."

This sudden announcement surprised us for a while. Kartik quickly handed over the mike to the coordinator and stepped down from the stage. I stood up from my seat and walked towards the auditorium door where I was joined by Kartik.

We looked at each other with curiosity and walked swiftly towards the Headmaster's office. We knocked at the office door and asked for his permission to enter.

The Headmaster signaled us to sit down. He was giving some instructions to someone over the telephone; meanwhile the peon who was already present in the room handed over an envelope to him and left the office. The Headmaster looked towards Kartik and said in a concerned tone, "Kartik we received a phone call from your mother; you will have to leave immediately to your home."

After thinking for a while, Kartik asked the Headmaster, "Sir, I don't think I will be able to get a railway ticket to Mumbai at once. Did my mother mention any specific reason?"

Sir replied, "I am not completely aware of the situation, but on the behest of your mother, I have arranged an air ticket for you and a taxi to drop both of you at the airport. Here is your air ticket."

"Airport" I mumbled in surprise.

Headmaster said while looking at me, "Hurry up, Satyam you will accompany Kartik to the airport. Go and pack your stuff as taxi will be here in next 15 to 20 minutes."

We hurried our way to the hostel room. I helped Kartik in packing his stuff and we were almost done by the time taxi arrived at the hostel gate. Kartik appeared to be in a very pensive mood and an expression of worry was very much evident on his face while on our way to the airport.

I said while trying to assure him, "Things must be fine at your place."

Kartik gave a shallow smile but said nothing and kept looking thoughtfully out of the window. In an hour, we reached the airport. Kartik checked in and I returned to the hostel in the same taxi.

Upon reaching the hostel, I decided to go straight to the Headmaster's office to update him. The office door was ajar and I could easily see him standing in front of his room's window and looking thoughtfully through it. Entrance to the school, hostel, mess and almost entire school ground was visible from this window.

I knocked at the door and asked, "May I come in sir?"

"Come in" the Headmaster replied (without looking back).

I entered and stood in front of his desk. He said after giving a quick glance at me, "Did Kartik reach airport on time to catch his flight?"

"Yes Sir" I replied. I looked at my wrist watch and said, "He must be airborne by now."

Out of curiosity, I asked the Headmaster, "Sir, can I ask you something?"

Headmaster turned towards me and said, "I know, you want to know why Kartik had to leave in such haste."

He signaled me to sit down on a chair positioned next to the window. Meanwhile, he was continuously gazing out of the window.

I also tried to look out of the window but was not able to find anything significant.

"Satyam, do you see this big old tree in the garden?" the Headmaster asked.

"Yes sir" I replied.

The question felt very absurd to me, as the tree was quite conspicuous.

He asked further, "Can you interpret anything from this tree?"

{What is there to interpret from a tree? What kind of question is he asking? Surely, I could not ask any of these questions from him. Therefore, I pretended to think of a suitable reply.}

Without waiting for my reply he continued, "Our life is just like this tree. The people, family and friends surrounding us all the time are like these leaves.

He walked towards the table to have a sip of coffee and returned back to the window along with his coffee mug and said, "During autumn, the tree starts losing leaves and it appears lonely and lifeless. However, things change with the onset of spring. The old leaves are replaced by new ones and soon the tree becomes rejuvenated with life, enthusiasm and energy. Similarly, when we lose someone very close to us, our life becomes dull and haunting. However, when we move forwards in life and meet new people, we gradually start to forget all the sorrows of past. Life becomes full of happiness and vivacity once again."

I was listening carefully because now his words were making sense to me.

He said while pointing towards the ground, "Can you see the gardener collecting the fallen leaves?"

I stood up and popped my head higher in order to see the gardener.

He continued, "Son, just like a good gardener, we should collect and retain whatever useful we can learn from our friends and people around us; disposing-off the rest of the clutter from our minds."

He was right in a way but he was yet to answer my question.

Before I could repeat my question to the Headmaster, someone started knocking at the door. It was a continuous knock; I could also hear my name along with the knocking.

It was Shreya knocking at the car window. I woke up and quickly opened the door for her.

She said while seating herself, "It's very cold outside."

"I am so sorry to keep you waiting outside dear" I said as I pulled up seat to upright position.

"It's alright; you opened the door on the second knock." Shreya said while rubbing her hands against each other.

She said further while looking at me, "You are also exhausted. You should have gone home to take some rest instead of waiting for me."

I replied, "This was far better than waiting for you at home and making phone calls repeatedly. At least we are nearby and together."

Shreya said while placing her head on my shoulder, "Love you so much."

I caressed her hair gently and said while turning the ignition on, "How was the day today? Hope the operation went fine."

Shreya said in a dull tone while reclining back on the seat, "The operation went as planned.......the patient is recovering. Over-all the day was fine."

I said while driving the vehicle out of the parking, "Okay, it means it was not good. Tell me what happened?"

She smiled and replied, "When did I say that? The day was fine."

I asked her again, "Oh, come on; tell me what happened."

Shreya turned on the car stereo in a low volume and said, "You are so stubborn. Ok, nothing worth mentioning happened but my H.O.D. always creates problems for me."

Shreya took out her cell phone from her handbag and said while checking notifications on it, "Well, I guess such things happen at one's work place."

I replied while speeding on the highway, "No, I don't think so. I think you need to sort this out?"

"What can I do Satyam?" she spoke in a low tone.

After thinking for a while, Shreya continued, "In few months, my residency period will be over and I will not have to deal with him anymore. So relax."

I said while taking the vehicle down from the highway to the service lane connecting our house, "The behavior which is wrong and abusive in any way must not be accepted, even for a moment."

Shreya said while putting her phone back in her bag, "You will not understand how things add up in our field?"

I smiled and said while parking the vehicle in our porch, "I understand everything."

I continued as I took her hand in mine, "Listen dear, you have reached this position due to your hard work, capabilities and relentless efforts. You are a doctor and according to me, such behavior should not be tolerated for even a single moment whether you are a student or an intern. No one has the right to create problems for others."

"What if he fires me or creates a much worse working scenario if I protest? You don't know how influential such people are?" Shreya asked firmly.

"Remember dear, people are not as petrifying as we make them to look; it is only in our imagination. When harm is coming either way, then it is far more prudent to face the situation with courage and put up a fight to maintain one's self-esteem and prestige" I replied with conviction.

We stepped out of the vehicle and after locking the car doors, I continued, "It is far better to leave and start something afresh than to lose your peace of mind, dignity and self-confidence to some scumbags."

We walked towards the main door of our house and I said assuring her, "Honey trust me, learn to raise your voice and treat yourself with the respect which you deserve. If anything goes wrong, remember you are not alone. I am just a call away."

We stepped inside our home after unlocking the door. It was around 12:30 a.m., so we freshened up as quickly as we could and slept after having a bowl of instant noodles.

Chapter—5

Cherish your life

The next morning, I was sitting on my bed facing the sunrays being showered on me from the windows. The sleeping duration was bound to be short but my better half was already up and was preparing breakfast in the kitchen. I could listen to her monologue and it was clear that she was upset by the kind of work environment at the hospital.

I got up and made the bed neatly. Then I took a shower hurriedly and walked to the dining room for breakfast after getting dressed up.

Shreya turned around after placing the serving plate of sandwiches and got surprised on seeing me ready for the office and asked, "Look at you! When did you get up? You are almost ready. I didn't want to wake you up this early."

I replied while picking up a slice of a sandwich from the plate, "You were busy preparing breakfast while I was having a shower."

While serving the breakfast, she kept forgetting one thing or the other on the table. It was evident that she was quite nervous for the upcoming day. We had discussed at length the previous night as to how to tackle challenging situations at one's workplace but I decided not to talk about it any further unless she speaks up on her own.

I said while pulling a chair for Shreya and sitting on the adjoining chair, "Come, let's have our breakfast and then I'll drop you to the hospital."

The dullness was evident on her face. Shreya constricted her eyelids and said while sitting, "It will take some time for me to get ready;I think you should leave for your office. I will go on my own."

I said in a neutral tone, "I am not in a rush today and moreover, don't want to be in the office before my staff arrives. So you can take your time, I will drop you."

"Are you sure?" she asked while looking thoughtfully through her weary eyes.

I smiled and replied, "Yes, finish up with your breakfast and get ready."

Shreya completed her chores, got dressed up hurriedly and we set off for the day's work. It is indeed difficult to let your loved one to face hard time. I felt like stepping down from the car on reaching her hospital and settle the issue with the H.O.D. once and for all but by doing that, I would have mitigated the only reason for which she might have learnt to stand up and fight for herself. Therefore, I controlled my anger and decided to let her take a stand for herself.

To me, it appeared as if she was having much more on her platter than what she could have handled. So I decided to start a conversation and asked her, "You still appear to be stressed out Shreya; will you able to manage your work at the hospital?"

She said while attempting to dodge the question, "No, I'm fine. Slight apprehension is obvious. "

I said while turning left with indicator, "Have I told you about Kartik?"

She thought over a while and replied, "Kartik....yes. You have talked about him a few times."

I said while fixing my gaze on the road, "We used to hang out in a café near our school. The coffee and the view from the café were splendid. You could easily see kids playing football and other games from the café.

One day, while sitting in the café Kartik said while looking towards a group of children playing football in the ground,

"Satyam would you like to listen to a story?"

It was an unexpected question.

I asked, "A story? Why not, go ahead."

Kartik started narrating the following story, "A small boy, little shy and tender, used to play football with other children in a park. Whenever the ball would come to him, a big fat boy would bully him down and snatch away the ball every-time. The little fellow would cry and soon he developed a profound fear for the game. Now, he would start crying on the very sight of the ball coming towards him. His cries were in anticipation that soon the big fat boy will come following the ball."

Kartik continued and said, "Once a wise old man observed this and he walked close to that little boy and said while squatting down near him, "Son, instead of running away and crying, you should stay and enjoy your game even if you don't get the ball. If somebody keeps on bothering you, then you should not hesitate to fight back and inform an elder person. Always remember that no one is superior or stronger than you and no fear is bigger than the man himself. There is nothing to be afraid of in life. You cannot leave the game simply because someone is bothering you."

(I glanced at the rear view mirror; Shreya was listening attentively to me).

So I continued and said, "Shreya, likewise I also believe that one should not allow anyone to rob off your smile and self-confidence. Stand for yourself and fight back. Instead of nurturing the fear and the feeling of dejection, it is always better and wise to face the trouble with grace and confidence.

Let the anger accumulate inside you; so that you have enough energy to uproot the cause of your problems. No matter whether you win or lose but at least you should stand up for yourself."

I stopped the car in front of the hospital's gate and said after unlocking the doors, "Will meet you in the evening."

I looked at her; she was still looking thoughtful.

I said before leaving, "Shreya, if your schedule permits we will plan something for today's evening."

Shreya smiled and waved good bye.

I turned the car and headed straight to the office. On my way back to the office, I was thinking about Kartik and the story which I had just narrated to Shreya. I entered my office, pulled my chair to sit and soon my memories dragged me back to the Headmaster's room where I was sitting on the chair placed near the window.

I repeated my question to him, "Sir, why did Kartik have to leave in such a hurry?"

Headmaster said while looking at the falling leaves, "His father suffered a heart attack and unfortunately he died this morning."

He continued while keeping his gaze fixed outside the window, "This news could have probably caused a lot of trauma to Kartik. Therefore, I decided not to tell him or anybody else about this unfortunate news."

I was shocked but that day I learnt something that stayed in my mind forever. We don't cherish the life when we have time in our hands. At that moment, we behave in a manner as if it is never going to end. Till hours ago, we were having the best time of our lives and now in a fraction of second, things have changed forever.

I was sitting alone in my hostel room trying to introspect and ponder over the issues pertaining to uncertainties of life. One thing is sure that time does not stop for anyone, it simply keeps on moving and so does life.

The final exams were approaching therefore, all of the introspec-

tions, lessons and teachings were left behind in the pursuit of completing school syllabus on time.

One day, while I was preparing for my exams, the peon came to my room and informed, "Satyam, the Headmaster sir is calling you in his office."

I asked curiously, "Why? What happened?"

Peon said, "I don't know why. But he said that it's urgent."

"Hope nobody else has died this time" I thought while getting up from my chair.

I reached the Headmaster's room and knocked at the door. "Sir, may I come in please?" I asked.

He replied while signaling me to take a seat, "Yes Satyam, come in."

There was a boy sitting in front of the Headmaster. I thought that he might be a new admission.

As I advanced further to take seat, I was surprised to see that the boy who was sitting was Kartik.

The Headmaster said while looking at me, "Kartik is planning to leave the school."

I asked shockingly, "What? But why? We are just a month away from the exams. Don't do this Kartik."

Kartik replied in a shallow voice, "I know but my circumstances do not permit me to continue. I will have to leave."

The intensity of agony that he underwent was clearly evident through his face and he was appearing quite weak.

There was a pin drop silence in the room for a moment.

I wanted him to stay but was not able to understand how to persuade him to change his mind. I was not able to get over with the fact that my only friend was about to leave the school forever.

I paused for a while to control my emotions and said hesitatingly, "If you are quitting because of financial problem, please don't do that. I can easily cover up for all of your expenses."

Kartik smiled and said while controlling his emotions too, "I am happy to have a friend like you. I am not leaving due to financial reasons but there are some other responsibilities back at home which need my attention."

The Headmaster sir said in a concerned tone while handing over a document to him, "Kartik, here is your school leaving certificate. However, if you ever need any guidance or help in future, please feel at ease to contact me."

Kartik thanked the Headmaster and both of us moved out of the office.

He started walking towards the school gate instead of the hostel room.

"Are you not coming to our room?" I asked him.

Kartik replied, "No friend, taxi is waiting at the school gate. I will have to rush."

"Alright then, I will accompany you" I said.

We started walking towards the school gate.

I asked while looking at him, "What about your stuff? When will you come to collect it?"

He replied while placing the letter given by the Headmaster in his pocket, "Please donate them."

"Donate them?" I asked surprisingly and thought over a while. "Sure, I will" I said.

I asked thoughtfully, "But are you sure? Do you really want to leave? I mean, how and from where would you continue schooling?"

Kartik did not reply to my question but kept walking.

Sensing that he will be gone forever, I mustered up some courage and spoke, "Kartik, I am sorry for your loss."

Kartik took a gulp down this throat and said while taking a deep breath, "What can be done, this is life. Although, I miss my father but will have to bear with his absence."

"Can I ask you something?" I said.

Kartik smiled and said, "What is it?"

I asked reluctantly, "How are you able to behave in such a relaxed and composed manner despite of being in such a grave situation?"

Kartik replied while looking thoughtfully, "Once I had underperformed in a test due to which I felt very dejected and confined myself most of the time in my room for days. Noting my depressed state of mind, my father counseled me that life is not meant to be imprisoned behind closed doors of remorse and grief. Life is all about learning, exploring and resurrecting in front of challenges laid down by the destiny. There is no bravery in running away because the person who runs away from challenges is never able to see what exactly the life has planned for him. One can never succeed in life by running away from the adversities; no matter how hard and harsh they may seem."

I was busy processing the vast amount of information which Kartik was showering over me. I was listening to him with full attention and wanted to hear more of it.

He continued, "The most important point that my father had told me was that our destiny may not be in our control, our future may not turn out to be what we expect but one thing which is under our absolute control is our thoughts which guide our actions. Never undermine and never underestimate your inner potential because most of the times we are not aware of our own strength."

By now we had arrived at the school gate where taxi was waiting for him.

He said while opening the taxi door, "Don't worry about me. I will keep in touch."

I said while hugging him, "Sure, we will stay in touch."

In another moment, he was gone forever and that was the last time we got the time to interact with each other. Thereafter, neither I received any letter or call from him nor was I able to spare time to contact him. However subconsciously, he was always somewhere in my mind.

I could hear a buzzing sound; it was my secretary on the

intercom calling to remind me about my lunch with a client who was interested in setting up a bottling plant in Himachal Pradesh with us. I thanked her for reminding me and disconnected the call.

Thereafter, I decided to call Shreya to check on her. I picked up my cell phone from the table and dialed her number.

Amazingly, the call was answered promptly. This does not happen usually.

"What a pleasant surprise; I am hearing you this early instead of your caller tune" I spoke.

Shreya said candidly, "Miracles do happen sometimes."

I asked her eagerly, "Is everything all right?"

Shreya took a deep breath and said, "I had some heated discussion with the H.O.D. today and to my surprise, my name is no longer in the duty roster."

"Good for you" I said happily.

She paused for a while and continued skeptically, "Not sure about that. But I am free this evening and most probably in the evenings to come."

"Alright, will pick you up at 5pm" I said.

Shreya replied, "Ok, bye for now."

"See you in the evening" I said and disconnected the call.

In the evening when I reached her hospital, she was already standing in front of the hospital gate. Sighting our car, she waved at me.

I unlocked the door and Shreya quickly hopped inside.

"I can't wait to hear the details from you"I said.

Shreya placed her bag on the back seat and said, "It was not a smooth day but I am feeling a bit relieved now."

"What happened?"I asked inquisitively.

She replied, "In the morning, I met Neeta at the reception where she informed me that this time my duties according to the duty roster prepared by the H.O.D. are either long shifts or are placed during odd hours."

"What did you do then?"I asked while steering my way on the road.

Shreya replied, "After verifying what Neeta told me in the reception, I decided to discuss this with the H.O.D. and therefore I immediately walked towards his room"

Shreya continued while taking out her phone from her bag, "I was so infuriated that I entered his cabin without knocking or seeking his permission. He was enraged to see me walking in without asking for his permission. However, this time unfazed by his anger, I directly came to the point and asked him to explain the weird schedule fixed for me on the duty roster."

"What happened then?"I asked.

Shreya continued, "He did not expect this kind of behaviour from me. Unable to give a logical and a prompt answer to my question, he shifted the blame on some clerical error. He assured me that he would take strict action against the administrative staff for such kind of error in printing. I don't know how I became this courageous but I told him sternly that I am not going to do any of these irrationally assigned duties and he should refrain from unnecessarily harassing me."

Shreya looked at me and said, "After all this drama, I walked out of the room and went straight to the cafeteria. I was trembling. After having a glass of water, I realized what I had done. For a moment, I got scared but then I decided not to be. However, this proved beneficial to me."

"How did it so?" I asked while steering vehicle out of the highway to the service lane.

Shreya replied while gently stroking her hairs with her fingers, "After an hour, a new roster was issued and amazingly without including my name in it. I knew that the H.O.D. is trying to play me but I totally ignored his tactics. Neeta suggested discussing the matter with the administrative office but I refused."

Shreya said while tying her hairs, "I knew he was cooking up something and I was right."

"What was it?" I asked while looking at her.

Shreya replied while searching for house keys in her bag, "Nothing. One of his favorite interns came up and informed me that instead of the rotational duty, I have been assigned an indoor patient by the H.O.D."

I said while parking the car in the porch, "This appears to be a good bargain."

Shreya placed her bag on her shoulder and replied as we neared the doorstep of our house, "No, I could sense trouble in this."

I said in order to cool off the matter, "I think you unnecessarily doubt him. May be he got startled by the manner you dealt with him in the morning."

Shreya unlocked the door of our house and said, "Not at all. He is a highly manipulative and an egoist person."

She placed her bag on the sofa and continued while washing her hands in the wash basin, "The patient allotted to me is a difficult person to handle as per hearsay and he must have done this deliberately."

I hanged the car keys on the key holder and asked, "Why so?"

Shreya wiped her hands after washing them and said, "I think, I should freshen up first and then we'll talk in detail."

She walked towards the bathroom to have a shower; meanwhile I picked up a watering can and started watering the plants placed in the balcony and in the kitchen garden.

This time Shreya took a little longer than the usual time under the shower. I always felt that bathroom is the most preferred place where our thoughts like to interact with us in an uninhibited manner. After a while, Shreya walked out of the bathroom wearing a bathrobe and asked as she saw me uprooting the weeds from the flowerpots, "Why don't you change and freshen up quickly?"

Removing the gardening gloves from my hands, I replied hastily, "I am going....just give me a minute."

After freshening up, I walked to the kitchen where Shreya was busy preparing dinner. On seeing me entering the kitchen she kept the knife on the chopping board besides the diced vegetables and said while switching on the coffee machine, "That was quick".

I smiled and asked her, "So you were telling something about your patient earlier. What was it?"

"She is aged, must be in her sixties and is suffering from a very severe heart ailment. Above all, I have heard that she is highly uncooperative and fussy." Shreya replied while placing the coffee mugs and a bowl of fries on the serving tray.

"Don't worry, everything will be fine" I assured.

I picked up the serving tray, placed my arm around her shoulder and said as we walked towards the living room, "Just because the case has been assigned to you by your H.O.D after that argument, it does not mean that you need to be so apprehensive."

We settled ourselves on the sofa and I placed the tray on the table. I held her hand gently in mine and said candidly, "Cheer up, you idiot."

Shreya gave a slight frown and handed over the coffee mug to me. I took a sip and found that sugar was missing in it but did not dare to complain.

I added further in order to encourage her, "I fail to understand that how can anyone work with a maverick like your H.O.D. I mean who assigns a doctor to look after only one patient like a nursing staff. Well, even if he did it, still you should try and discharge your duties to the best of your knowledge."

I continued and asked her, "Tell me; what would you have done if that patient had approached you in the O.P.D?"

Shreya thought for a while and replied,"You are right."

She took a sip from her coffee mug and the bitter flavor of the coffee brought an expression of irritation on her face. She said while placing the coffee mug back on the tray, "Oh, just a minute; I will be back." She got up and walked to the kitchen to bring some sugar."

Shreya said after adding sugar in both the mugs, "It's not worth anticipating anything. Let us wait for the dawn."

I said, "See, you just sorted out the matter by yourself. Just go and meet her tomorrow morning with a fresh mind. Treat her to the best of your knowledge and abilities."

Thereafter, we had a light conversation over the dinner. I woke up from sleep in the middle of night to check on her and was happy to see her sleeping peacefully.

Chapter-6

Importance of family

Next morning, after reaching the hospital, Shreya entered the special ward. She wished her newly assigned patient and checked her vitals. After finding some of the readings to be normal, Shreya was about to head towards the doctor's duty room to prepare a new case study file when her patient suddenly called out, "Doctor, if you don't mind can I ask you something?"

Shreya turned back and asked in a concerned tone, "Yes Mrs. Vasudha, what is it?"

Mrs. Vasudha said while trying to reposition her intubated hand in the reclined position, "Doctor, would you mind spending some of your valuable time with me if you are not too busy?"

"Sure....I can" Shreya replied while wondering what might be the issue.

Shreya seated herself on a chair placed besides her bed.

The patient continued, "I am feeling a bit low since morning. My attendant is also not here that is why I am bothering you like this."

"It's alright Mrs. Vasudha. We all come across a low phase in life at some point of time. You can discuss whatever is engrossing your mind."

The patient started narrating her life's account in a concise form. During the conversation, Shreya came to know that Mrs. Vasudha is a prominent social worker and is engaged in various philanthropic works.

Shreya was disappointed to know that except for her husband, the rest of her family members were not very supportive of her during the testing phase of her life.They had not visited her even once after her admission to the hospital and this ignorance on the part of her family was making Mrs. Vasudha feel dejected.

After listening to her account Shreya spoke up, "I don't know what has happened to our society; why people tend to neglect their parents and elders when they are in need of utmost care?"

Mrs. Vasudha took a deep breath and said thoughtfully, "It will be selfish on my part to squarely blame my children for this."

"Why so?" Shreya asked disapprovingly.

She replied, "I have been involved in various philanthropic works for a considerable period of my life. It won't be wrong to say that I have spent most of my life doing charity. It is not possible to help the needy from the comfort of our home, so I had to visit places quite often. I used to be away from home for days and sometimes even for weeks together."

After a brief pause she continued, "In this quest of helping the needy and underprivileged, I somehow failed to spend quality time with my kids especially when they were young and needed me the most. Unfortunately, at that point of time they had everything in their life except for their mother."

Mrs. Vasudha continued with an effortful smile on her face, "I know it's too late for realization as my children have already learnt to live without me. Well, what can be said as it's not their fault; they have learnt what I have taught them."

Shreya was listening to her patiently.

Mrs. Vasudha grew teary eyed and continued, "Whenever they came to show me their little achievements or some trivial school projects which were important for them, I was always too busy to pay attention to what they had to share with me. It was their nanny who always looked after them during my absence and even in my presence...sometimes. I attained a good position in the society but at the cost of my family."

Shreya said while interrupting, "But you were working to earn for them."

Mrs. Vasudha replied in a fatigued voice, "Was it so? I mean how much money does a child need to secure his/ her future? It's bare minimum. What a child needs the most is care; affection and continuous attention by parents which we failed to give them.

I have realized that little kids have a very fine sense of judgment and they know well how much a person, whether a relative or a caretaker is concerned for them. My kids must have also learnt this but in a hard way. Barring few instances, they never complained for my absence and gradually they learnt to live without me."

Mrs. Vasudha asked while looking into Shreya's eyes, "Now tell me that how I should squarely blame them for not being able to spare time for their ailing mother when I had never rescheduled even a single appointment or cancelled a tour for them when they were young. All that they had with them were a lot of toys, dresses, exotic holidays and a nanny."

She continued, "The truth is that I was running day and night to fulfill my own ambitions and to build a flourishing future for myself. They never asked any of this from me."

She turned her head towards a bouquet of flowers placed near the window and said, "Indeed I am successful but not completely."

Mrs. Vasudha turned towards Shreya and asked, "If you don't mind me asking; are you married?"

Shreya replied, "Yes, it's over two years by now."

Mrs. Vasudha continued, "Please don't let your family fall behind in your quest of success. Trust me, at the end of the day it's your family which matters the most and it cannot be replaced with any amount of money or luxurious facilities." Mrs. Vasudha glanced at the wall clock and continued, "I am really sorry for wasting your time with this lengthy conversation."

Shreya replied assuring her, "Not at all ma'am. It is better to speak about thoughts that cause pain to us instead of harbouring them.

Shreya turned her attention towards the case sheet she was holding and said, "I have to enclose this sheet in your case file and discuss about your condition with the H.O.D. So, I will have to leave now."

"Thank you doctor" Mrs. Vasudha replied with a faint smile.

Shreya walked hurriedly to the doctor's duty room and on her way she met Neeta who was heading towards the general wards.

Neeta asked while placing the medicine tray on the counter in the lobby, "Dr. Shreya is everything alright?"

Shreya replied, "I was supposed to submit my report to the H.O.D. before 11:00a.m. and it's already lunch time. I am yet to start preparing it and this delay might give him another chance to be angry."

Neeta replied, "The H.O.D. has gone to attend a seminar today which is scheduled to be held till 3 p.m. I think you are having ample amount of time with you to complete the report and submit it."

"You just saved my day. Thanks a lot." Shreya said while gently patting Neeta's shoulder.

"This is how I am, will see you later doctor" Neeta replied as she smiled and walked away taking the medicine tray along with her.

Shreya walked into the doctor's duty room, took out Mrs. Vasudha's record and said to herself, "Oh my God, look at the size of this file. I guess these people are treating this file and not her."

Shreya read the file and was in total disagreement with the line of treatment. After thoroughly studying it, Shreya took out a new file, prepared entire case details with treatment plan afresh and tagged the new file with the old one.

Shreya looked at her wrist watch; it was 2:40p.m. She smiled and said to herself, "Good, now I can have my lunch in peace"

The H.O.D. returned to the hospital at 3:15 p.m. and Shreya was already waiting outside his office along with the case file. He looked sternly at her in the waiting area but unfazed by his tantrums, Shreya wished him confidently and spoke further without waiting for his reply, "Sir, I have prepared case details of the new patient allotted to me."
"Alright; come in." the H.O.D. said while entering his room.

Shreya followed him and placed the file on his table. He opened the file and signaled her to sit.

After reading the new report, the H.O.D. asked sternly, "So Dr. Shreya, it looks like that you don't agree with the line of treatment planned for this patient. Quite possibly, you think that the doctors who have worked out and followed this treatment are incompetent."

"I did not mean to imply this, Sir" she replied.

"Then what do you mean?" the H.O.D. asked while flipping through the new case sheets that Shreya had attached.

Shreya replied assertively, "This is my observation and I don't think I have commented on anyone else's level of competence in my report. I have written what I felt appropriate for the patient placed under my supervision."

Shreya continued in a determined voice, "I fail to understand that why is she under observation without any active intervention. She should have been operated immediately on admission but I don't know the reason for which it has not been done yet."

The H.O.D. replied irritatingly, "Don't you know the complexity of procedures and the level of preparations which are involved in this case."

Shreya said, "Sir it's already a month, how much more time do we need to prepare and analyze. If this is beyond our competence, I think we should refer the patient instead of making her suffer."

The H.O.D. replied scornfully, "Oh you should be better off as a lawyer. Trust me."

"Thank you for suggesting Sir but I definitely know what I should be" Shreya replied while getting up from her seat.

She continued, "Sir, I have submitted the report as per my findings and observation. I will take back the file tomorrow morning; thank you sir."

After completing her statement, Shreya walked out of the room without waiting for any response from the H.O.D. It was already half past five; so she decided to leave for home.

In the evening when I returned from the office, I was happy to find Shreya in a good mood. I quickly freshened up and walked to the kitchen.

Shreya asked while serving me a glass of water, "So, how was your day?"

"It was fine", I replied.

After having few gulps of water, I asked, "How was your day with the new patient?"

She replied promptly, "The day was good and unexpectedly she turned out to be a humble lady. After interacting with her at length, I came to know that she is a noted philanthropist."

"That's good", I replied

I continued as we moved to the living room, "How is she doing?"

Shreya replied while seating herself, "Not good."

"Why, what happened?" I asked while sitting beside her.

"She is suffering from a severe cardiac condition which involves a very complicated heart surgery" Shreya replied.

I sipped on to my coffee and said after placing the mug on the table, "So, when is the surgery planned?"

Shreya replied, "There is no such date; not at least in my knowledge."

"What do you mean?" I asked surprisingly.

She continued, "I studied her case file today in detail. She is undergoing treatment in our hospital since one month and ideally she should have been operated way back but they are not operating her."

"Have you discussed this with your H.O.D.?" I asked.

Shreya replied, "Oh I had a fully blown argument with him today on this topic."

"Argument...what is there to argue about in it?" I asked astonishingly.

She replied, "He wanted me to toe the line which I refused to do and then like always he tried to overpower and humiliate me but I gave him a befitting reply. I made him clear that I am going to do what is best for my patient's recovery."

Shreya thought for a while after having a sip of coffee and spoke further, "I really don't feel like working there anymore."

I placed my hand on her shoulder and said, "Do what your conscience allows you to. However, I'm happy that you stood up for what you believe in."

Shreya smiled and said, "This is one of the advantages of having an intelligent, optimistic and a supportive spouse like you."

"So, what will you do now?" I asked.

Shreya replied, "I know one such charitable institution located at around 150 kilometers from Shimla which specializes in heart care. Almost every type of advanced and complex surgeries is performed there. One of my friends has completed her internship from there. I will recommend that institution to her tomorrow."

"What if she refuses?" I asked.

"It's the patient right to decide the hospital from where he/she wants to undergo the treatment" Shreya replied confidently while placing her mug on the table.

""What if the hospital authorities come to know about this referral?" I asked.

"I don't give a damn to what they think" she replied with conviction and looked thoughtfully through the window situated on the wall besides the sofa.

I smiled as I looked on at her and was quite happy to see this confident, assertive and all out version of otherwise gentle, caring and tender Shreya. It is rightly said that a woman has many personalities imbibed in her. I could very well sense that this was the new dawn in Shreya's life.......our life.

Shreya picked up the serving tray and said while moving towards the kitchen, "Dinner is already prepared. Wash your hands and I'll quickly serve the food."

Thereafter, we had our dinner and went to sleep.

Chapter-7

Stand by your decisions

Next morning while driving Shreya to the hospital, it appeared to me as if she has finally learnt to let go off the things and move forward.

I asked her while steering through the way, "So, have you made up your mind?"

"Regarding what?" Shreya asked while scrolling through her mobile phone.

"About referring your patient to that specialized centre for surgery" I replied.

"Oh, yes...yes.....definitely. This is the first thing that I will do this morning. It will be good for her." Shreya said while putting her cellphone back in her bag.

"Good", I said while negotiating a curve. After few minutes, we reached her hospital. I dropped her and continued towards my office.

Shreya walked directly to her patient's room and greeted her, "Good morning Mrs. Vasudha."

"Good morning Dr. Shreya" Mrs. Vasudha replied in an effortful tone.

Shreya asked her, "How are you feeling today?"

"As good as yesterday; maybe it's due to my age or the nature of my ailment but I don't feel any significant improvement in my health." Mrs. Vasudha replied wearily.

After checking the patient's vital signs, Shreya said, "Lately, I have been studying extensively on your condition and it can be cured with a very specialized operation but unfortunately that kind of expertise, I don't think this hospital has".

The old lady said with an effortful smile, "Yours is the best hospital around. Now tell me, what can be done? Do I need to go abroad?"

"I don't think so. There is a reputed charitable cardiac institution in the state of Himachal Pradesh. The institute happens to have the best team of cardiologists on their panel including some visiting doctors from abroad and not to mention the state of art facilities which they have." Shreya replied.

Shreya continued, "If you suggest, I can discuss your case with them."

Mrs. Vasudha thought for a while and enquired, "I have never heard about it earlier. Where is it located, doctor?"

Shreya replied, "It's around 150 kilometers from Shimla; apart from the infrastructure and medical expertise, the institute is located in the vicinity of beautiful mountains. The nature as we know has always been instrumental in healing; we just need to embrace it."

"Yes indeed." The old lady replied thoughtfully.

After thinking for a while she asked in a concerned tone, "Don't you know that suggesting such an alternative may perhaps go against you. What if your hospital management comes to know about this?"

Shreya placed her hand on the patient's shoulder and said in a firm tone, "For me, proper treatment and quick recovery of my patients is far more important than anybody's opinion or any policy".

She pulled a stool for herself and continued while sitting, "Mrs. Vasudha, I think you should consider about this. I will just share the details of the hospital with you so that you can check their credentials and all other details on their website. Actually one of my friends has completed her internship from this institution; therefore, I happen to know a little about that place."

Shreya shared the details with her and said after getting up from the stool, "Please let me know about your decision but don't take too long because I think that this surgery must be performed at the earliest."

The old lady's face lightened up and she said, "Your concern is appreciable. I will discuss this matter with my husband as soon as he reaches here after procuring the prescribed medicines and will let you know within an hour."

"Sure" answered Shreya.

Thereafter, Shreya walked out to head towards the doctor's duty room. While sitting in the duty room, Shreya took out some of the files of other indoor patients and started studying them.

After almost an hour one of the interns came up to her and said, "Good morning Dr. Shreya, the H.O.D. is calling you to his office urgently."

"Alright" Shreya said while getting up from her chair and headed towards his room.

Shreya knocked at the door which was already ajar and entered the room.

The H.O.D. closed the case file on which he was working while Shreya seated herself.

"Well Dr. Shreya, it appears that your hard work and sincere suggestions are of no use" The H.O.D. spoke in a sarcastic manner.

"You were already unwilling to accept any of them but Sir may I know the matter?" Shreya countered him calmly.

The H.O.D. replied with a grin, "I think your patient is not happy with the treatment which you are providing. Her husband has just requested for discharging his wife from the hospital. They are planning to visit abroad for her treatment."

He continued insolently, "Oh, I think we'll have to find a new patient for you. Your each and every minute is valuable, I can't even think of keeping a dedicated doctor like you without a patient to cure."

Shreya gave a shallow smile and said, "Sure Sir, you will find an ailing soul. Is this all or.....do you have any instructions for me?" Her response was quite contrary to what the H.O.D. had expected after inciting her.

"Oh no...no....nothing much, you may leave now" the H.O.D. replied as he reclined on his chair.

Shreya stood up and left the room.

Shreya headed straight towards the special wards to her patient's room. She entered the room where she found her being assisted to sit up by her husband.

"Mrs. Vasudha, I am so glad that you made up your mind. Trust me; you will not regret this decision because you require an immediate surgery" she spoke confidently.

"Had you not intervened, I don't know how much more I had to suffer here. Thanks a lot doctor." Mrs. Vasudha replied.

Shreya continued, "I have not done anything significant for you till now. Would you mind me asking from where would you undergo further treatment? You don't need to reply if you don't want to....it's really not necessary. I simply asked out of curiosity."

Mrs. Vasudha looked at her husband and replied, "From that very institute which you had suggested earlier."

"The institute indeed appears to be a reputed one and in order to get the best treatment; I would definitely want my wife to get admitted there as soon as possible" the patient's husband replied.

"But the H.O.D. just informed me that you have planned to go abroad for the treatment" Shreya asked surprisingly.

Mrs. Vasudha replied, "It was just a way to keep you out of trouble. It would be very kind of you if you can discuss my case with the doctors at that institute so that we can move ahead with my treatment."

"Sure...just give me a second" Shreya said while taking out her cell phone from her pocket and stood by the room's window.

She dialed the institute's number; the phone kept ringing for long but the call was not answered. Shreya dialed again and this time the call was answered just before it was about to get disconnected.

"Hello; is this the charitable cardiac institute?" Shreya asked.

"Yes it is. Please tell me how can I help you", asked the person on the other side of phone.

"I am Dr. Shreya from New Delhi and I am seeking for an admission of a heart patient at your institute....Thereafter, Shreya briefly described Mrs. Vasudha's health status to that person and requested for an early appointment. After asking few more details, he scheduled the appointment for Friday morning.

Shreya thanked him and asked further, "Sir, would you mind sharing your details with me, so that we know whom to contact once we reach there."

"I am K. Saxena, the coordinator of this institute and you can note down my mobile number" he replied.

Shreya noted down his mobile number. Thereafter, she thanked him and disconnected the call.

Shreya turned towards Mrs. Vasudha and her husband who were looking anxiously at her and said while scribbling on a piece of paper, "Here is the address of the institute and the mobile number of the Coordinator. He sounded quite humble and cooperative to me. You can also save my number; I will be in touch. Hope you will get the best possible treatment and get well soon."

Mrs. Vasudha kept the piece of paper in her purse and noted Shreya's number on her mobile phone. After saving her number she thanked Shreya.

"I am happy that I could be of any use." Shreya replied.

She said while placing her pen in the pocket, "Today is Wednesday; so you must think of starting the journey to Shimla tomorrow if you want to avoid night journey. Travelling to the hilly terrain will not be a problem if you book an ambulance with life support facilities.

"We will most probably leave tomorrow morning" the patient's husband replied.

Shreya wished them and left the room.

As expected, no other patient was allotted to Shreya till the evening. She kept reading case files in the duty room and when she was about to leave for home, Neeta informed her that the H.O.D. had placed her on operation theater duty without assigning any specific duty days.

Shreya said confusingly, "What is this? I have never heard of such a duty schedule before."

Neeta replied worryingly, "I don't know what to say but please don't lose hope; things will soon turn out to be better".

Shreya said while placing her handbag on her shoulder, "I will talk to him over this matter tomorrow. There is no need of further brainstorming. I am leaving for today; bye."

Neeta nodded and waved back at her.

On her way to home in a hired cab, Shreya was thinking about her patient. It occurred to her that Mrs. Vasudha might have not been able to do much for her kids but she had worked day and night sacrificing all her comforts to bring smile on the faces of countless needy people. She had served the unprivileged section of society at the cost of her family ties. After going through these series of thoughts, Shreya decided to help her patient in every possible way.

In the evening while having dinner, Shreya spoke up, "Satyam, I think I must accompany my patient; what do you suggest?"

"Can you elaborate please?" I asked while adding salad to my plate.

Shreya replied, "I want to accompany her to the charitable cardiac institute which I had recommended her."

"But why would you do so? She's not your relative. I don't think you have done this earlier?" I asked inquisitively.

I continued, "Is she in need of some sort of assistance?"

"In order to explain my decision, I'll have to narrate you her life story till now" replied Shreya.

I said, "I think I am having time to listen to you?"

After discussing each and every detail of Mrs. Vasudha and her family with me, she concluded, "That is why I have decided to accompany her. Both of them are an elderly couple and they would be reassured if I being her treating doctor till yesterday go with them and explain her case properly to the senior doctors at the charitable institute. Moreover, it's me who has recommended them this charitable institute and I always wanted to visit that institute but never got the chance to do so."

Shreya continued after swallowing the morsel of food, "It would be far better to learn something new than to remain idle and face humiliation here."

"I admire your spirit to help others. You must go but have you discussed this with your patient?" I asked having done with my meal.

"I wanted to inform you before calling her" Shreya replied.

"Sure, you must call her" I said.

After completing the dinner, Shreya picked up her mobile phone and called Mrs. Vasudha to express her willingness to accompany her.

She was elated to know Shreya's decision and thanked her.

After disconnecting the call Shreya turned towards me and said, "Satyam, they are quite relieved now but will you be able to manage office and home in my absence."

"Don't worry I will manage" I replied assuring her.

I continued and asked, "How have you planned your journey, shall I drop you?"

"No…. it would make your schedule quite tough to manage as you would be back to your workplace after two days. You just hire a taxi for me and I'll join the patient's ambulance on the way." replied Shreya.

I said, "That's ok, but don't hesitate to call me if you need any-thing. In fact you can also seek help from my parents if need arises as our home is only at a few hours distance from that institute."

"Sure, I will" replied Shreya.

After a little pause, she said while smiling, "Thanks for under-standing and supporting me."

"It's alright Shreya; this is what companionship is all about. I think we should quickly finish the chores as you need some rest before embarking upon a new journey in the morning" I replied.

Next morning, Shreya set off for the treatment of her patient, Mrs. Vasudha at the charitable cardiac institute in the remote hills of Shimla in a taxi.

Thereafter, I also freshened up and left for my office.

Chapter-8

Defining success

It was a very demanding week at the office but was good for the expansion of our business. Finally after putting in a lot of efforts and time, our team was able to convince a very reputed investor to invest in our new mineral water bottling plant, which I was planning to establish in the hills of Narkanda in Himachal Pradesh.

The investor had given an appointment for the coming Monday and as he was not willing to come to Delhi; therefore, the meeting was scheduled to be held in Shimla.

While at the office, the time used to fly away but once I reached home, everything would feel stand still and silent.

This was the first time when Shreya was away from home. Although we were constantly in touch with each other but I was missing her badly. That day, I learnt the importance of the proximity of loved ones in life. I often used to become irritated by her constant chattering but today I was missing it the most, especially in this profound silence.

Upon reaching the institute, she informed me that she had

been provided a free accommodation. I was surprised on knowing this but did not probe further as she was comfortable in staying there and moreover, I never doubt her decisions.

Shreya updated me regularly regarding the progress of her patient and about what all new she was learning there. She was motivated by the new technologies and the techniques employed at that institute.

After reaching home, I called her up but the call was not answered. Perhaps, she might be busy.

I placed the cellphone on the table and started looking for the television remote but wasn't able to spot it. While I was busy looking for it, my cellphone starting ringing.

It was Shreya. I quickly received the call and said, "Hi. How are you?"

"I am fine. Have you reached home?" asked Shreya.

"Yes, few minutes ago" I replied and asked while still looking for TV remote under cushions, "How is your patient doing?"

Shreya replied, "Her operation is successful. She will recover soon." Sensing that I was not listening attentively, she asked in a curious tone, "Satyam, you appear to be somewhat busy."

"No.....no nothing like that; was just looking for the TV remote" I replied.

"Did you look for it in the keys shelf?" She asked.

I walked towards the key shelf and was relieved to find the remote. "How did you know about it" I asked surprisingly.

"Will discuss this later" She replied as she giggled.

I said while switching on the TV, "Shreya, I am planning to visit Shimla this Monday for a meeting with an investor."

Shreya replied, "That's good. You are quite proficient in making deals. So you will be here day after tomorrow."

"I will reach by Monday evening and will come to meet you after the meeting concludes." I replied.

"Alright, let's see how our schedule permits us to accompany each other. I miss you a lot" she said.

"See you soon dear. Take care" I said.

After disconnecting the call, I made an online booking in a five star hotel at Shimla as I was not willing to disturb my parents unnecessarily for this short trip. Like always, I prefer to make prepaid reservation for hotel room as I don't like standing in queue to clear dues at the time of checkout.

Monday morning, I hired a taxi and was able to reach the airport on time. The flight was also on time. I get a sense of relief when things go as per the schedule. After about half an hour's journey, I landed in Shimla and hired a taxi to the hotel. On my way to the hotel, I called up Shreya to inform her about my arrival. It was just 9 a.m. in the morning when I had reached the hotel and as the meeting was scheduled at 12:00 p.m.; I therefore decided to take some rest.

Thinking about the possible outcome of the meeting, I lay down on the bed and closed my eyes to take a nap. Before I could catch some sleep, my secretary called me up and informed me that the client has requested for a change in place of the meeting. Instead of Shimla, he wanted to hold the meeting at Narkanda, where one of the proposed sites of the plant was located. However, the time of the meeting was not rescheduled.

I must tell you, some of the investors behave in a manner as if they are not only investing in your project but are also buying you along. They don't consider the comfort, opinion and situation of the other party concerned. What can be done? If you want them to invest money in your project, you have to abide by their decision and so did I.

Without wasting a minute, I called for a taxi and immediately started my journey to Narkanda. The roads were jam packed and it took me almost two and a half hour to reach the destination. I was famished; therefore I decided to have a proper breakfast before the meeting.

The investor reached the venue exactly at 12:00 noon. It was an intensive meeting and he was very meddling in questioning. Finally after a lengthy discussion, he consented to invest in our project.

Now this was a great step forward in the growth of my company.

After the meeting was over, I glanced at my watch and the time was half past two. The charitable institute was not too far from the meeting place; therefore instead of going back to the hotel, I decided to visit Shreya. I asked the taxi driver, the one I had hired since morning, to head straight towards the institute. On the way, I informed her about my travel to her location.

Due to excessive traffic jam on the main road, the driver suggested to take a detour. He said, "Sir, I think we should take an alternate route. Although, it is a bit longer but we will be able to save at least half an hour."

"No problem, take any route which you find appropriate." I said while looking at the traffic.

The journey was going smooth until the taxi had to stop with a heavy jolt. "What happened; can't you drive carefully?" I asked sternly.

The driver replied with uncertainty, "I don't know. It looks like, the engine has stopped working."

Vehicle's machinery should be checked properly before plying it on the road but it was useless to argue with him and so I asked while stepping out of the vehicle, "Is it repairable?"

"First, let me check." He said while opening the bonnet of the vehicle.

The driver said after quickly inspecting the engine of his vehicle, "It appears to be something major; I will have to tow the car to the workshop."

I asked while looking at the lonely highway, "Do you know any service station nearby?"

The driver took out his cell phone from his pocket and said while dialing a number, "There is one, a few kilometers away. I will call some help and they will be here in no time."

Unable to connect the call, he checked his phone and said disappointingly, "It appears, there is a network issue. This area has a problem with mobile signals."

I checked my phone but there was no network either.

The taxi driver managed to stop and convince one of the taxis plying on the highway to tow his car to a nearby workshop. On reaching the workshop, the mechanic informed us that the vehicle needed an engine overhaul and it would take at least 2-3 hours to become roadworthy.

"Is there any taxi stand nearby?" I asked him.

"No" replied the driver.

After thinking for a while I asked, "Can you arrange another taxi from here?'

He said while locking the car, "It would be difficult but I can arrange"

"Why difficult?" I asked.

The driver replied while looking at the highway, "I can't contact anyone over the phone; therefore I will have to look for a vacant cab on the highway."

"How much time will it take?" I asked restlessly.

He replied in a helpless tone, "I am not sure but it may take an hour or more."

The driver walked besides the road looking for vacant cab whereas I started taking a stroll in the opposite direction. I was walking aimlessly on the road after a considerable period of time.

While walking towards a curve, I caught sight of a huge sign-board placed on a nearby hilltop through which a flight of stairs ascended into the woods. The signboard read "Welcome to 'The Humble Abode'- A place to be in unison with your mind and soul."

The driver was few meters away from me; therefore I beckoned him over to speak to him. He walked swiftly towards me.

"I'll wait till your taxi gets repaired. It's already 6 p.m. by now, so I think by morning we might be able to continue our jour-ney to the charitable institute. Can we get a lodging facility for this night at this place?" I asked while signaling towards the signboard.

The driver replied thoughtfully, "This is an ashram at the hill top but I don't know whether they provide lodging or not."

I said, "I think you should go and confirm."

He nodded and started walking towards the gate which was at a distance of about 200meters from the road. "Wait" I called out."I will also come along with you."

As we approached the gate after climbing up the stairs, we were lucky enough to spot a person wearing saffron clothes. He was appearing too young to be a sage but going by his attire and a divine calmness on his face we decided to address him as Swamiji.

The driver was quick to react; he said while greeting him with joined hands, "Swamiji, we are travellers and our car broke down on the way. We would be grateful if you let us in for a night."

Swamiji asked, "Where were you heading to?"

He replied, "Swamiji, we were on our way to the Longforest area."

Swamiji said, "It's alright. We all are in need of help at some point of time. Just go straight towards the reception, the volunteer sitting behind the counter will guide you."

After instructing us, Swamiji left and we followed the directions given by him to reach the reception. The ashram premises were very neat and tidy. The receptionist noted down our respective phone numbers, addresses and placed a copy each of our identity proof in his record register. Thereafter, he led us to a small cottage through beautifully maintained meadows. The cottages were located on either side of the meadows.

I was truly amused with the vitality of the surroundings and felt much relaxed. Truly, nothing can live up to the healing power of the nature. On entering the cottage, I was delighted to find two bedrooms, a sitting room and a washroom equipped with all facilities. I lay down on the bed to take some rest and as the bedding was quite comfortable, I fell asleep at once.

I woke up in the evening at around 7:00 p.m. feeling relaxed and energetic. I walked out of the cottage to take a stroll. While walking through the ashram premises, I observed that it was a well-maintained setup with all the basic amenities including a medical centre fully equipped with all of the latest life support facilities and a resident doctor.

There was a dedicated part of land for cultivation of herbs and various medicinal plants. I was surprised to find out that some of the volunteers engaged with cultivation were students of botany. I got a chance to have a little interaction with them; all of them seemed to be quite sincere and intelligent.

Going by the size of the ashram land and the level of the infrastructure, I was feeling inquisitive to know more about it.

Luckily, I spotted the very same saint or Swamiji. I walked towards him and asked, "May I meet the manager of this magnificent place?"

He smiled and replied, "Sorry, we don't have a manager here."

I glanced around and asked further, "Then how do you run this place so efficiently on daily basis?"

He replied, "With the guidance of our Guruji, charity received and of course with the help of people who volunteer to work here."

He said while watering a plant, "Look around you; you are surrounded by a lot of them. These people come here in search of peace of mind."

"Can I meet your Guruji?" I asked him.

He replied while refilling his watering can, "Right now he is in the Longforest area."

I asked inquisitively, "Do you have another branch there?"

He seemed amused by my question and said while continuing watering the herbs, "No we don't have any branch. We are running a charitable hospital there."

I responded promptly, "It's a very noble initiative for the well-being of the society."

He continued and said, "Our Guruji started with this institution 7 years ago as his personal getaway. Gradually, after interacting with the local people of this hilly terrain and pilgrims, he came to know about the various difficulties that were faced by them. This ashram and the hospital at the Longforest are his contribution to the society."

I asked thoughtfully, "Swamiji, I am seeking answers to few questions which often torment my mind. Would you be kind enough to enlighten me on those issues?"

He replied while sitting on the grassy area besides the pavement, "Only if I have the right answers with me."

I asked as I sat on the ground in front of him, "Why is it so difficult to be happy even after attaining success in life?"

He replied while placing the bundles of herbs on the grass,

"Happiness is not a separate entity but it is a collective outcome of success and the ability to recognize your success. To understand this, first we'll have to understand **'success'** because happiness is invariably related to it. Success itself is a very personalized type of feeling and its definition varies from person to person. For some people material success is important whereas for others spiritual aspects are far more important than any other achievement in life. Therefore, it won't be wrong to say that you are successful only when you feel the success from your heart; otherwise, no achievement is big enough to call for celebrations.

In reality, every person whose income is sufficient to take care of him and his family needs is professionally successful. You should be successful in your eyes because it is your life and it is you who actually knows what is best for you."

Swamiji said while looking towards the horizon, "One more thing; the basic mantra for a happy and successful life is - 'Never compare'. Always cherish what you have and always remember that everyone gets his or her due share of success in life; we just need to stay focused and keep working. The common motive of everyone's life should be to build a good character and not to be the one running in a rat race."

Contrary to the expected lengthy looped speech, he was concise yet precise with his words.

He was right; there is no parameter defining success. We are successful only if we can feel it; otherwise, we end up struggling no matter how much we achieve in our life. When we indulge in habit of comparing, no feat of ours appears to be big enough to call for celebrations.

I looked at my life retrospectively and realized how this habit of comparison had robbed happiness from my life and never allowed me to cherish any of the successful moments. I topped in my school but was unhappy to get second position in the zone. I was meritorious in MBA entrance but was still unhappy as I could not get admission in my preferred college. I started with my own business at an early age but still unhappy as I could never receive the best businessperson award.

In this never-ending quest for success, I not only lost touch with my family but also lost my best friend; the only one that I ever had. I had promised to be in touch with him but never bothered to contact him even once.

Life endowed me with various occasions to celebrate but I was never able to recognize them. It took me so many years and a journey to this forest to understand that success indeed is a very personalized type of feeling. You are successful only if you can appreciate it.

Success has no specific criteria, requirement or specification. In fact, it is the most customized thing in world; which changes form and definition as per one's perception, need, circumstances and efforts. Unfortunately, we seldom realize this and keep on running in a rat race.

Swamiji picked up the bundle of herbs from the ground and stood up to conclude the topic by saying, "It is the quest of our mind which forces us to seek answers." Thereafter, he headed towards a glasshouse of medicinal plants.

I stood there for another few minutes to experience the tranquility that prevailed after the little discussion with Swamiji.

After taking a stroll for a while, I glanced at my watch; it was quarter to 8pm. So, I decided to look for an eatery. While searching for it in the premises, I came across the ashram's mess which was quite decent and hygienic.

The dinner was already ready by that time, therefore instead of snacking I preferred to have dinner.

Having done with it, I took out my mobile phone and called up

Shreya while taking a stroll in the beautifully lit garden.

"Hello Satyam. Where are you?" she asked.

"The taxi which I hired in the morning broke down on the way. Fortunately, I was able to find a suitable lodging place in the otherwise deserted road. I will start my journey to your institute tomorrow morning" I replied.

Shreya said, "I was worried for you. You should have called me earlier."

"This area has very feeble network coverage, and therefore could not contact you earlier. Your voice over the phone is cracking while conversing right now. So, I will call you in the morning before leaving" I replied.

"Sure, take care" she said.

"Ok, bye", I said before disconnecting the call.

Shortly, I was joined by the driver.

"Sir, the car has been serviced and we are good to go now" he said.

"Good, we will leave early tomorrow morning. If you had been particular with the maintenance of your vehicle, we would have been saved from this unrequired halt" I said.

Chapter-9

Listen to your inner voice

Next morning, I was woken up by the chirping of birds which was quite loud yet pleasing. The streaks of sunrays filtering through the thick branches of the trees enlightened the room. It was awesome; the splendidness of the nature is difficult to describe in words. These are best experienced by self.

The driver was already up and had gone to wash his taxi.

I quickly freshened up and walked out of the cottage. I took few deep breaths and decided to jog a little. Half way through the jogging track, I noticed a huge gathering in the middle of a big lawn. I was surprised by looking at such a huge gathering so early in the morning.

After completing a round of the track, I became a little tired as I wasn't a regular jogger. Therefore, I made myself comfortable on a bench along the sidewalk. While checking my cellphone for the messages and mails I overheard somebody preaching. Frankly, I don't prefer listening to such philosophical speeches. Initially, I ignored it but then out of curiosity; I tried listening to some of it. This was the first time I was listening to any preacher.

The part of speech which I overheard was-

"We all are faced with different challenges in our lives and in order to move ahead, we need to overcome these challenges. However over a period of time, while facing them on daily basis, we forget about updating and refreshing ourselves to attain best form of ourselves. In our already overbooked schedule, we find it difficult to take out some time for ourselves or engage in the activities which can rejuvenate us. Gradually in a much mechanized lifestyle, we start losing our own self. We start losing that person who can laugh, who loves adventure and most importantly who knows how to forgive and move ahead in life.

Unfortunately, most of us have lost that person from our individuality. We are left with an egoist aching self which feels threatened, neglected and keeps on justifying our own acts even though how irrelevant they may appear. All of this leads to an endless suffering to which most of us are exposed to.

He said further convincingly, "It is the quest to end this suffering which motivates us, prompts us and forces us to act. Look at yourself; it is the quest of your unrelenting mind to seek answers which has made you come to this place and that too this early in the morning.

It is all within us. We all know the solutions to our problems but seldom believe in our inner self. Our inner voices are so muzzled by our ambitions and peer pressure that they are not at all audible to us. Even if, somehow we manage to listen to our inner voices, we don't trust them.

We don't trust them because we never learn to trust ourselves. Instead of trusting our self we rely on others. The habit of dependence never allows us to take decisions on our own."

He said this rightly. The habit of dependence is so deep rooted in us that we always ignore what our inner self is trying to tell us. We always seek guidance from others and follow them irrespective of the fact whether the guidance or suggestions given are suitable for us or not.

I glanced at my watch, it was already 8 am. Although I wanted to listen more of him but I was running a little late on my schedule, therefore I got up from the bench and walked towards my room to get ready for the journey ahead.

On my way back to the room, I was thinking about what I heard a few moments ago; it was enlightening. His concept of becoming the best form initially made me to laugh but this was the most appropriate thing we need to do and become better in life. Just become as better as you can and keep on improving yourself just like any sophisticated electronic device which keeps on updating to provide efficient and effective service. In other words we simply need to redefine ourselves. I must have met him in person, if I had a little time to spare.

I freshened up, got ready and went straight to the mess to have my breakfast where the taxi driver was already having his meal. By 9 am we were ready to start with our journey. At the time of departure, I met Swamiji at the reception with whom I had a little enlightening conversation yesterday. I greeted him and said, "Swamiji, good morning?"

He greeted back and replied, "You look all cheered up and a lot happier. Hope you had a pleasant stay at our ashram."

I replied while completing the checking out formalities, "It was great indeed but may I ask you something?"

"Sure, go head", he replied.

I said, "In the morning, I heard someone preaching. May I know who was he?"

"He is our Guruji" he replied.

I said after clearing the payments (which were unrealistically nominal, it felt like everything was almost for free in the ashram), "He was great....although, I could not listen to him at length but whatever I heard him speaking, it was thought provoking an meaningful. I would be delighted to meet him personally, if he is okay with that".

Swamiji said while handing me a magazine, "He usually has a busy schedule. However, if you liked his vision then take this along."

I took the magazine from him and said surprisingly while flipping its pages, "What? A business magazine; I didn't know that your Guruji takes interest in business."

Swamiji replied, "Our Guruji is highly qualified and an experienced person. He writes regularly for many business magazines and this issue also contains few of his recent articles. May be, it can be of any use to you."

After completing all the formalities, I thanked Swamiji for providing us accommodation for the night and left.

In next few minutes we started with our journey to the Longforest area. I took out my mobile phone and called Shreya. This time she was quick to answer.

She said, "Hello, how are you Satyam?"

"I am fine, how are you? Pack you stuff, I will be there in few hours." I said.

She replied, "All done, just waiting for my dear husband."

I smiled and said softly, "Will be there soon dear."

I disconnected the call. After placing the phone back into my pocket, I picked up the magazine which the Swamiji had given me and started flipping through its pages to find the article written by Guruji.

I smiled at my foolishness when I realized that I forgot to ask the name of his Guruji. I started glancing through the pages of book until I came across a quite unique article "Has your company HR lost the human touch?"

The title was catchy enough to raise the curiosity. I looked for the name of the writer but it was published under the name of an institution 'The Humble Abode'. I thought to myself that this must be the article which Swamiji was talking about in the reception.

I started reading the article and it went like this-

"It is often complained by the managers that the staff working for them is not efficient and dedicated enough but have we ever tried to find the reason for the same?

To understand this better, we simply need to start with recalling the recruitment process to know how these inefficient people got hired.

These people were hired by you and that too after subjecting them to a rigorous selection procedure. They were selected only after they outshined rest of the applicants and met the selection criteria laid down by your company.

Now a question arises; how do these selected people who were then considered to be brilliant get transformed into so called inefficient baggage?

If you ever get the time to notice, majority of the workers working under you can be classified into one of the following three types- meticulous, confrontational and to the point worker.

The meticulous type of worker will come early and would never refuse to work late whenever asked for. He/ she would work with full sincerity, dedication and commitment. For them, presence or absence of the supervisor does not make any difference. He/ she would think many times before applying for leave or requesting for any favor.

The confrontational type of employee is the one, who is pivotal in office politics. He/ She knows how to work but will only deliver in presence of the supervisor to get appreciation. If the supervisor is absent, then that working day is like a holiday for them. Forget about giving additional work; you cannot push them even a little to deliver the assigned task on priority. He/ she knows how to transform a petty issue into an argument. For them every trivial personal matter is far more important than any official proceeding.

Let us talk about the third type of worker- 'to the point type worker'. He/ she is exactly as per the name. He/ she is self-motivated, performs the work with full sincerity and dedication but he/ she will not pull on with additional work; especially when they are sure that this additional work will not only compromise their routine but will also affect their personal time. They do not hesitate to argue with their boss or senior if they find something wrong. Most importantly, he/ she is not the yes-sir type of employee.

The problem is not with your workers but it lies with you and so is the solution. It is a normal human tendency to avoid arguments and unpleasant atmosphere at work place. Therefore, most of us avoid giving work or additional responsibilities to the confrontational type of employees and instead, we start asking the other two types of employees for that piece of work.

Gradually when this becomes a routine practice, sensing the undue liberty given to the confrontational employee; the "to the point" type of employee starts refusing any additional work assigned to him/ her. In a way, that employee is right in refusing this additional work as it is not appropriate on the part of the manager to overburden an employee while sparing the other and that too without any justifiable reason.

Since the work cannot be delayed, we start diverting that work to the first type of employee, i.e. the meticulous type.

With this additional task, the already overburdened employee fails to deliver and at the end of day, we call him as inefficient and an unproductive member.

I would like you to introspect. Do you still think that you are being troubled by your employees? The person working for you is very much human. So if possible, try to deal your employees with a human touch."

The article was indeed an eye opener. His vision was clear, comprehensible and above all- acceptable.

For the first time, I realized how hardworking my secretary and some of the staff members are. Still, I keep on scolding them. I was feeling bad; partially, because of my unsympathetic behavior towards my staff and mainly because I had fired Nikita, an office assistant, just few days back because I was finding her inefficient and inept.

Unfortunately, she was just another hardworking but meticulous type of employee who got stumbled in front of excessive work load. It was my duty to address her problems and grievances when her performance had started to decline. May be I should have talked to her or counseled her but instead, I kept on scolding and finally fired her for inefficiency.

Today, I realized why my father always said that success is a team sport and to win you need to have a good team. In a business, the manager is the captain and a good captain always treats his teammates prudently. People work with sense of responsibility if you trust them, praise them for their efforts and forgive them if they have done some petty error. On the contrary, I was unaware of the troubles faced by my staff. I do not remember any moment when I had genuinely appreciated anyone.

Now, I decided to build my office culture afresh in accordance with the vision of my father. To begin with, I decided to re-hire Nikita as an HR executive with increased responsibilities and salary. I knew that she and my secretary, Ishika were good friends therefore I took out my cellphone and called my secretary.

Ishika quickly answered the phone. After getting updated on the office work I asked, "Are you still in contact with Nikita, our former office assistant?"

She replied apprehensively, "Yes, we talk few times. What happened sir?"

I said, "If I remember correctly, she had a degree in management."

"Yes sir, she had one." Ishika replied.

I said further, "Please contact her and ask her to resume duties from the next morning as an HR associate, if she is willing."

"Sure sir, I will do that" she replied happily.

Before I could disconnect, my secretary continued, "Sir, I don't know what made you to change your mind about Nikita but certainly by doing this you have pulled her out of the miseries as she is facing a financial crunch. She will be indebted forever."

"Ishika, just inform me after contacting her" I replied.

She said, "Sure sir, thank you sir."

I disconnected the call and placed the phone inside my coat's pocket.

I never had this notion that a little decision of mine can have such a deep impact on someone's life. I glanced at the magazine which I was holding in my hands and said to myself, "I surely need to meet this wizard, at least once."

I placed the magazine on the seat beside me and pulled the car window all the way down to feel the cold breeze. Still a journey of over an hour was left to reach the Longforest area.

Chapter-10

Be assertive

It was an exquisite villa; the sunshine peeping through its majestic wooden windows was making it vibrant and cozy. The windows were draped with big white vintage curtains which were being swayed constantly by a gentle breeze flowing continuously through the partially open windows.

Soft music was playing on the radio at a soothingly low volume in the living room. Shreya was busy packing her stuff as she was about to leave the institute in about an hour. With little to pack, she was done quickly with it. After packing, she placed her luggage in the drawing room and moved out of the villa carrying a book in her hand. She sat on the porch stairs and started reading the book.

Shortly she was joined by Srishti, an intern at the institute. They greeted each other and she seated herself besides Shreya.

Sensing her uneasiness, Shreya asked, "Srishti, what is the matter? You look stressed out. Do you want to discuss something with me?"

"Oh, nothing of much importance; you must be busy right

now" replied Srishti.

Shreya said, "It's alright Srishti; tell me what is it?" She closed the book which she was reading and continued, "I was just utilizing my spare time."

She said, "I am having an interview scheduled next week so I am a little nervous about it."

"It's quite obvious to become nervous before putting your skills to the test. This happens with everybody, it's absolutely normal" replied Shreya.

"This is the reason, I approached you. I am finding it difficult to manage my anxiety and don't know what to do. I fear, I might mess up the things for myself" Srishti replied thoughtfully.

"Ok, I will tell you how to prepare yourself for an interview. Just listen to me carefully" Shreya replied.

"I am all ears" Srishti said with eagerness.

Shreya continued, "Interview is one of the most complex words I have ever come across. A word capable of generating overwhelmingly mixed feeling of opportunity and fear often obscuring our minds."

"Very true" Srishti replied.

Shreya continued assuring her, "An interview is just an attempt made by the recruiter to look deep inside you; to assess and explore your potentials which they can utilize in further development of their business. However, you must not forget that they are also looking for your weaknesses too."

"That goes without saying" Srishti replied thoughtfully.

Shreya said while cheering her up, "Just relax; there is absolutely no need to have any paranoia about it. All you need is to focus on your abilities and skills instead of mugging up in the name of preparation. You and your capabilities are the most vital assets for any recruiter. So focus on that."

Srishti was listening very attentively. Shreya continued, "Now, I will tell you how to face an interview."

"Sure" she replied while expressing her keenness to learn more from Shreya.

Shreya said, "The best way to face an interview is to interact with the interviewer as if you are interacting with your own mirror image with nothing to hide, nothing to boast about and above all nothing to fear of.

Before appearing in an interview, visualise yourself in the chair of the interviewer and ask variety of questions from yourself. If you have any sort of CV handicap, like break in experience or lesser experience or lack of expertise or any other thing that may possibly pose hindrance in your selection; then make it sure to prepare a comprehensive and convincing reply about your CV handicap. Selectors often ask such questions invariably in an interview which often turn out to be detrimental to the chances of your success. If you can convince yourself with your replies then trust me, you won't find it difficult to convince the selectors."

Srishti said regardfully, "Thanks for sharing your knowledge with me. Your guidance has already abated the anxiety levels in me. Is it all or do you have something more to add to it."

Shreya laughed a little and said, "I think there is one more thing which you should know and that is never lie in your interview. Even if they try to highlight your shortcoming or mount pressure on you, don't give up. Instead, try hard and give them the best possible reasons to appoint you."

Shreya placed her hand on Srishti's shoulder and continued, "Every interviewer likes to judge your willingness to work and perseverance to attain your goal. They often look for stuff like willingness to walk that extra mile etc. It does not matter how

THE QUEST FOR REDEFINING ONESELF

you perform in the interview but you should never behave like an underdog; always maintain your dignity and confidence".

Shreya got up from the stairs and said further, "The only difference between you and the people sitting on the other side of the table is that they have already proved their worth and now it's your turn. Therefore be fearless, do your homework, have faith in your abilities, face your interviewer gracefully and reply confidently. Success will be all yours.

It's your self confidence and trust on your abilities which matter the most. People's perception about you is immaterial and it keeps on changing with time."

Shreya concluded while looking at Srishti, "I think that will be all."

Srishti stood up and thanked Shreya while saying, "Dr Shreya today you have surely changed my concept and perception of interview. I will be ever grateful for your guidance and the ingenuousness with which you shared your knowledge and wisdom with me."

Shreya wished her good luck for her upcoming interview and Srishti left after thanking her again.

Shreya walked inside the villa to give one final look to ensure that she did not leave behind any article belonging to her and waited patiently for my arrival.

Chapter-11

Redefine yourself

I was about to reach the institute, so I took out my mobile phone to inform Shreya. She asked me to come directly to the place where she was lodging and gave me the necessary directions up to the place. In few minutes, I reached the location.

I stepped out of the car at the porch and told the driver to stay put. However, the driver wanted to have some refreshment so he left for a nearby eatery after assuring me that he will be around. After the driver left, I climbed up the porch stairs.

I pressed the doorbell of the villa.

Shreya answered the door promptly. She was all dressed up for the journey, looking pretty like always.

I closed the door behind me and asked, "Dear, How are you?"

Shreya hugged me firmly and said cheerfully, "Now I am feeling good. You can't imagine how much I missed you."

I replied while gently caressing her hairs, "I know....I also missed you but what I missed the most was your cooking, coffee and most importantly your nonstop chatter."

Shreya giggled in response and said while tying her hairs into a bun, "I can prepare some coffee for you if you want and meanwhile you can freshen up."

I looked at my watch and said, "Sure, it appears we are having some time with us."

By the time Shreya prepared the coffee I took a stroll inside the accommodation.

We seated ourselves in the drawing room and she handed over the mug to me. I smelt the coffee as I held on to the coffee mug and said, "Oh I missed this aroma. Hope this time you have added sugar."

Shreya giggled and asked, "How was your journey?"

"Life changing" I replied instantly.

"How is that so?" She asked inquisitively.

I replied while placing my arm around her shoulder, "Those few hours that I spent in that ashram or....you can say.....was fortunate to spent, changed my vision towards life and helped me to reconsider my priorities."

Shreya gave an expression of surprise on hearing this. She

asked further, "What are you saying? I was of the notion that you don't like such places......."

I said interrupting her, "For the first time, I got an opportunity to meet the people for whom money is not everything. It would be more appropriate to say that for them money is just another commodity."

Shreya was listening curiously as she was not accustomed to this facet of my identity. It was all new to her.

I continued, "I'm happy that you decided to help your patient; otherwise, I wouldn't have got the opportunity to visit that ashram and would have spent many more years of my life chasing insubstantial and fallacious things."

Shreya said with a sparkling smile, "I am glad to hear this."

I said while placing the mug on the table, "Tell me how was your experience and how did you end up in this enchanting place?"

Shreya replied, "When we reached here, there was no receptionist to attend to us. When nobody turned up even after a while, I dialed the Coordinator, Mr. K. Saxena's phone number and spoke to him. He apologized for the absence of the receptionist and deputed a person to attend to us."

"That sounds quite professional to me" I said.

Shreya continued, "That's not all; in the evening he came to visit Mrs. Vasudha. There I got a little chance to interact with him and during that interaction we came to know that he is also the owner of the institute. He prefers to remain easily available for the general public; therefore he uses the coordinator as his designation."

Shreya said further after placing her coffee mug on the table, "He appreciated my efforts and genuine concern for Mrs. Vasudha. I also told him about you and your business ventures. Before leaving, he offered me this accommodation for lodging. As I had already explored the accommodations available locally during the day time, all of them were inappropriate. I found this villa to be suitable as it is located within the hospital premises; therefore, I agreed to stay here."

Shreya checked the time on wall clock and continued, "I need to deposit the keys of this house at the reception. We can also wish speedy recovery to my patient at the institute before leaving. So, I think we should move now."

I took out my mobile phone and called up the taxi driver. After the taxi arrived, I took the luggage to the taxi and placed it in the boot space while she locked the main door of villa.

On reaching the institute, we met Shreya's patient who was admitted in a special ward on the first floor. She was looking all cheered up and was doing well. We wished her a speedy recovery and also shared a light chat with her husband Mr. Ramcharan before leaving.

On our way to the reception, I said, "I think I should personally thank the Coordinator for assisting you and your patient?"

"This seems to be a good idea" Shreya replied after handing over the keys to the receptionist.

I asked the receptionist, "Hello, can we meet Mr. K. Saxena?"

The receptionist replied, "Sir is not here. If there is any urgency, you can call him on his mobile phone. I can give you his number."

"It's alright. Can I leave a thank you note for him?" I asked.

He said while giving me a paper and an envelope, "Sure, you can."

I asked while straightening the folded edge of the paper, "Can you please tell me his first name?"

He replied hesitantly, "I am afraid, I can't help you with this. I have joined here recently and have never heard anyone using his first name while addressing him. The entire staff addresses him as Mr. Saxena or Coordinator sir."

I quickly penned down a thank you note on the paper and said while closing the envelope, "Please don't forget to hand this over to your Sir."

He replied calmly while placing the envelope in his table's drawer, "Sure sir; have a safe journey ahead."

We walked out of the reception and started with our journey.

On the way, the driver said while glancing at me in the rear view mirror, "Sir, this institute has helped a lot of needy people."

"Yes indeed", I said.

Thereafter, it was more of a silent journey. Shreya was sleeping where as I was looking at the beautiful landscapes en-route. I decided to visit our home in Shimla for few days before going back to Delhi. In few hours, we reached our destination.

My mother was elated to see us when she opened the door.

We touched her feet to seek her blessings. She hugged us happily. She said while wiping her tears, "I was just thinking about both of you while cooking."

"Where is Dad?" I asked after seating myself on sofa.

She replied while reaching out for her cell phone, "Your father is busy in a meeting at his office. He will be here soon. Or let me call him."

Shreya said, "Please don't tell Dad about us, we would love to surprise him."

Mother approved of her plans and asked Dad to come early.

She asked, "I don't understand that why are you travelling with such a little luggage?"

I replied while smiling, "Mom you know that I don't carry luggage with me. This all belongs to Shreya."

Thereafter, Shreya narrated the entire episode of our journey to her.

Soon Dad reached home and rang the doorbell. I answered the door; I still remember the expressions of intense happiness which spontaneously spread across his face.

He hugged me and said, "What a pleasant surprise.......where is Shreya?"

Shreya walked out of the kitchen to serve tea. After placing the serving tray on the table, she touched his feet and took blessings from him.

I was content to see happiness on their faces. Although, this was a short tour which lasted for two days but the satisfaction of spending time with parents was immense.

We were ready to start with our journey to Delhi but the surroundings and pace of life at home town was so comforting and peaceful that a part of me never wanted to leave this place.

With pleasant memories, we returned to Delhi to resume our normal routine but with much improved personalities and point of view.

Shreya started working for Mrs Vasudha's charitable foundation on her request and the philanthropic work at the foundation gave a new dimension to her career.

I was also a reformed person with much friendlier and prudent approach towards my staff. Amazingly, now no one appeared inefficient to me. Nikita had joined back and was working with full enthusiasm. Business was as usual but the office was look-ing much livelier.

One Saturday morning, the doorbell rang. Shreya answered the door and received a registered post for me from the Longforest area. Shreya said surprisingly while looking at the letter, "It is from the institute at the Longforest area."

She said while opening the envelope, "It appears that my hus-band has received an acknowledgement for the thank you note that we had left with the receptionist."

As I was watering the plants, I requested her to read it out for me.

Shreya opened the letter and started reading it aloud.

My dear Satyam,

"I should have written this letter way back but unfor-tunately I did not know where to find you. Few years back, I had even visited our school searching for your address but couldn't find it as the old records of the school were gutted in a fire. So, I was left clueless.

Following the death of my father, the business suffered a

huge loss. That was not all. I was barely learning to handle all of that when I suffered another blow by losing my mother, leaving me shattered and all alone. It was my spiritual inclination which helped me to get through that phase of life. To escape the stressful city life, I built a small place for meditation in the hills which was subsequently termed by the local people who also used to visit it as 'the Humble Abode'.

It took me many years of hard work to restore, consolidate and bring the family business back on the track. In all these years of endless struggle and success, I never forgot to remember you even for a day because you were the only family I had left with me.

I still remember how desperately you tried to convince me to not to leave the school in the mid-session. You even accompanied me up to the taxi with a hope that you might be able to convince me to change my mind.

Life has its own means to part and unite people. Few days back, I received a phone call from a young lady who was quite annoyed with the mismanagement at my charitable institute at the Longforest area.

I addressed the issue immediately and instructed the institute's authorities to admit the patient.

While interacting with her, I came to know that she is a doctor who belongs to Shimla and is employed in a hospital at Delhi. I also learned that her husband's name is Satyam Sharma. On hearing the name, I obtained a few more details about you from her and then went straight to my office. I opened my laptop and searched for you with the help of provided details.

Oh dear, you can't imagine the happiness I experienced when your smiling face popped up on the screen under your company's name. I literally jumped out of the chair in jubilation. Finally ... I had found you. I was elated but I did not reveal my identity to Shreya as I wasn't certain whether she knew about me as your school friend or not.

Moreover, it has been over a decade since we met or talked to each other. Therefore, I preferred to remain silent on the matter. Please apologise from her on my behalf if she had faced any inconvenience during her stay at the institute.

It is a lot easier to pen down emotions than to express them verbally. That is why I preferred to write to you instead of calling. Shreya is already having my number with her. I will be waiting for your call."

See you shortly,

Kartik Saxena

This revelation sunk me into a deep state of reminiscence. I placed the watering can on the floor and took the letter from her to take a look at it.

I said thoughtfully while looking at the letter, "Kartik Saxena was my roommate as well as my classmate in the Convent of Hills. In-fact, he was my best friend. Unfortunately, he had to leave the school midway."

I continued, "The ashram which he is referring to in the letter happens to be the very same place where I had stayed for a night while I was on my way to meet you at the institute."

I continued overwhelmingly, "You would be surprised to know that apart from that charitable institute at the Longforest area where he is tending to the physical health of people, he also runs an ashram, The Humble Abode. He is doing his best to serve the community in every possible way. In fact, during my stay at the ashram I had heard someone preaching but I didn't know that the orator was Kartik. His words are still thought provoking, meaningful and captivating like they used to be."

I said as I shifted my gaze towards the horizon "Years ago, he had helped me in overcoming my shortcomings when I was young and naive. He trusted me even when I did not have much faith in my own capabilities and now after so many years he came out of nowhere to help me in redefining myself. I am happy for his progress and also impressed by his constructive role in the betterment of society."

Shreya turned teary eyed on listening to me and said while wiping her eyes, "I am glad that you finally found your best friend.

It is rare to find a friendship nowadays where such a selfless mutual regard exists. Now I know why I was offered such an extraordinary accommodation at the premises of the charitable institute; this explains everything."

I placed the letter safely in my pocket and put my arm around Shreya's shoulder as we beheld the sight of fully bloomed carnations.

Printed in Great Britain
by Amazon

14661403R00099